Gertrude, Gumshoe  Curse

ROBIN MERRILL

New Creation Publishing

Madison, Maine

This is a work of fiction. Names, characters, businesses, or-
ganizations, places, events, and incidents are either the prod-
ucts of the author's imagination or used in a fictitious manner.
Any resemblance to actual persons, living or dead, or actual
events is purely coincidental.

Cover by Taste & See Design

1

Gertrude sat in her recliner with Hail curled up in her lap. She would never tell the others, of course, but Hail was her favorite cat. They were watching *Antiques Roadshow*, but Gertrude had seen the episode multiple times. She was growing bored and restless, but she didn't want to get up, because she didn't want to disturb Hail. He was riveted by the 1923 New York Yankees-signed baseball on the screen.

Gertrude started fiddling with her phone. When she opened Facebook, she saw something that ejected her right out of her chair, sending Hail flying. She headed for the door, grabbing her walker almost as an afterthought as she fled.

Mere seconds later, she was pounding on Calvin's door. She opened it just as he said, "Come in."

"You won't believe it!" Gertrude said, breathless.

"What?" Calvin said without looking up from the television.

"That rascal Alec won the slam!" She fell onto Calvin's couch and immediately plunked her feet on the coffee table. Her legs were so short, they barely reached.

Calvin finally looked at her. "What? What slam?"

"The finals! He won the final slam! He gets to go to nationals!"

"Oh." Calvin paused. Then he said, "So?" and returned his attention to the screen.

"So?" Gertrude screeched. "So that's embarrassing!"

"To whom?"

"To me! To the entire state of Maine! That's who we're sending to represent us?"

"Oh Gert, he's not that bad. Besides, all the other poets are either dead or locked up in jail—what did you expect?"

Gertrude folded her short arms across her chest. "I should've stuck with it. I could've beaten Alec." She spoke his name as if it tasted bad on her tongue.

Calvin shook his head slightly, still looking at the television. "I'll admit, you were better at that poetry slamming than I thought you'd be, but I don't think you could've beaten Alec. And you need to let that go."

"Let what go?"

"Your dislike for that kid. You didn't like his hair, so you assumed he was a murderer. But he was just a kid with bad hair."

"I don't judge people based on their *hair*, Calvin. I judged him because he was a bad apple. A nasty, nasty, rotten apple." She took a deep breath and looked around Calvin's trailer. "We need a case. I'm bored."

"Don't you have any collections to alphabetize?" he said with sarcasm.

"No. I'm all caught up. Do you want to go lawnsaleing?"

"On a Tuesday? No one has lawnsales on Tuesdays, except those criminals who keep their junk on their lawns every day."

"Why are those people criminals?"

"Because they're trying to run a business from their yard, without buying a business license. Then we have to stare at their junk every time we drive by. Having to stare at the occasional junk sale is bad enough, but every single day? Enough already! If you want to run a junk store, open a store like a real businessman."

"You need a license to run a junk store?"

"You need a license for everything. Haven't we learned that?" Calvin was referring to Gertrude's recent arrest for investigating a crime without a license. He had hired a lawyer who had struck a deal with his buddy the DA.

This silenced Gertrude for a second. But then she said, "We could go to Goodwill? I need some new umbrellas."

"Speaking of that," Calvin said, ignoring her suggestion, "have you looked into what you need to do to get your PI license?"

Gertrude groaned. "Not yet. I'd rather go to Goodwill. Take me to Goodwill, and then I'll do my research when we get back."

"No deal. When do you start your community service?"

"I'm supposed to start Thursday." There was no enthusiasm in her voice.

"Well, you may not be excited, but be grateful. It could be worse. Community service is a lot more fun than jail time."

"I am grateful, Calvin. I really am."

Calvin looked at her, his eyes wide.

"I appreciate you hiring Stan to defend me, and I'm not even too shook up about community service—"

Calvin's phone rang. He struggled to climb out of his chair.

"Are your hips bothering you?"

He ignored her. "Hullo?" he said into the landline phone. Then, "Oh, hello!"

Whoever that is, Calvin is sure excited to hear from them, Gertrude thought, with more than a little jealousy.

2

"What was that all about?" Gertrude asked when Calvin had finally hung up the phone.

"Don't act like you don't know. You were hanging on every word."

"Every *other* word. Only hearing your end of the conversation made no sense. There's a haunted lake? Who haunts a lake? Who was that?"

"Melissa."

"Melissa haunts a lake? Or Melissa was the one on the phone?"

Calvin took a deep breath. "It was Melissa on the phone."

"Melissa calls you?" Last Gertrude had heard, Calvin and his daughter were estranged.

"Not very often." Calvin returned to his chair and sat down carefully. "Only when she needs money."

"I didn't hear her mention money."

"She didn't. Not directly. She probably would if she got desperate enough, but I won't make her come right out and ask. She was just telling me that she lost one of her cleaning jobs, so now I know she's in need." He reclined his chair with a wince.

"Calvin, what is wrong with your hips?"

He didn't look at her. "Just a little stiff is all. She was cleaning some joint on Clearwater Lake. The Happy Trout or some foolish thing. Now the guy's going to sell, and so he let her go."

"Can't she clean for the new owners?"

"I don't know, Gertrude."

"So what was all that business about a ghost?"

Calvin rolled his eyes. "Melissa has always had a wild imagination."

Gertrude waited for him to say more. He didn't. "Well, what did Melissa's wild imagination say about a ghost?"

"She said she wasn't too upset about losing the job because the lake is haunted." He barked a derisive laugh.

"How can a lake be haunted?"

"How should I know?"

Gertrude chewed on her lip, thinking. "We should go investigate."

He laughed again. "There's nothing to investigate, Gertrude. It's just an old story."

"Old story? I've never heard it."

"Yeah, well, you don't get out much."

"That's not true!" She was genuinely offended.

He looked at her, his eyes softening. "You're right. I'm sorry. I suppose you do get out quite a bit these days. But we still don't need to go investigate a lake."

"Let's just go pay a visit to The Happy Shark place."

Calvin laughed. "Happy *Trout*. She said it's a combination store, inn, and marina. Not sure what we'd do there. Unless you want to rent a boat."

Gertrude pulled herself off the couch. "If you don't take me, I'll find someone who will."

Calvin looked at her, seeming to weigh his options. Finally, he reached for his remote and turned the television off. "Just let me get my feet dressed."

"I'll wait outside." She headed out to the truck, but when she pulled on the door handle, nothing happened. So Calvin found her still standing beside the truck. "Why do you lock your vehicle in Mattawooptock?"

"I never used to until I started hanging around you," Calvin said. "I'm afraid you might attract a criminal element." He pressed a button on his fob, and the door clicked. Gertrude stowed her walker in the backseat and then climbed into the front.

"Not true. If anything, I *repel* the criminal element. I'd like to think they know to stay away from me by now."

Calvin laughed, and it made him sound younger. "Maybe."

As soon as Calvin started the truck, Gertrude reached down and turned on the seat warmer, even though it was eighty degrees out.

Calvin rolled his eyes. "I'll never understand how you can stand that."

"Feels good on my fanny," she said and rolled her window down.

He used the controls on his door to roll it back up. "Don't need the window down. We have air conditioning."

She pressed the button again. Her window started to descend, but he overrode it from his side. "I like fresh air!" she said.

"And I like to not throw gas money out the window!"

"Fine," she said, crossing her arms with a harrumph. "So how far away is this Silly Shark?"

"*Happy Trout*. And probably about forty minutes. I don't know for sure. I don't go that way very often. It's sort of out in the middle of nowhere, and on the way to nowhere. Not really close to any town. Probably how they stay afloat, selling milk to summer folk suckers for eight dollars a gallon."

"So what do we know about this haunting?"

"Only what Melissa told me, which wasn't much. Apparently there's this local legend that the lake is haunted by the ghost of some girl who died there years ago, and apparently recently some of the summer folk have heard some screaming at night or some foolishness. I'm not putting much stock in it."

"What do you have against summer folk?"

"They're not real Mainers. They just come up in the summer and clog our roads and crowd our beaches. It's one thing to do this in Old Orchard Beach, but they've spread inland too. I don't know where they all come from, honestly. Massachusetts, I guess ..."

Gertrude only partially heard these last few words. She was asleep.

3

The Happy Trout didn't look very happy. It was an enormous, sprawling building sandwiched between the road and the lake, making Gertrude wonder why they'd ever built a road so close to the water. Calvin couldn't find a place to park and started grumbling about summer folk again.

A monstrous three-dimensional wooden trout hung over the doorway to The Happy Trout. It had probably once been colorful, but the sun had faded its yellow speckles to a dull beige, and part of its tail had been chipped off. The building itself looked worn and weathered, but it was still a lively place. As Calvin and Gertrude approached, a group of barefoot children spilled out the front door with ice cream cones.

"They're going to get plantar warts," Calvin grumbled.

As they passed under the wooden trout, Gertrude gazed up at it nervously. "That thing is going to fall on someone and crush their noggin."

Gertrude blinked rapidly as her eyes adjusted to the dim indoor lighting. They were looking at what appeared to be a small country store, with mostly bare shelves. A woman was scurrying behind a counter, over which hung a fairly extensive menu that stretched from fried clams to banana splits.

Calvin stepped up as though he'd been there a thousand times.

"Be right with you!" the woman said cheerily.

"No hurry," Calvin said with equal cheer.

"Why the sudden mood swing?" Gertrude asked, stepping up beside him.

"Because they have dynamites."

"What?"

"You know ... dynamites! It's on special." He pointed to a paper plate that hung on the wall. Someone had written on it in black marker: Homemade Dynamites $5.99.

"What's a dynamite?"

He looked at her. "You can't be serious."

The woman stepped up to the counter. "What can I get for ya today?"

"What's your name?" Gertrude asked.

"Isabel."

"Hi, Isabel," Gertrude said. "Tell us about this haunting—"

"Never mind that," Calvin snapped. He looked at Isabel. "Sorry about my friend. She's a nut. We'd like two dynamite specials, please."

"I don't want a dynamite!"

"Yes, you do," Calvin said, handing a twenty over the counter to Isabel.

"If you'd like to pick a drink out of the cooler—" Isabel said.

"We'll just have tap water," Calvin said.

"I don't want tap water!"

"Then you can buy your own drink," Calvin said, and pushed his twenty closer to Isabel.

She took it, her eyes flitting between the two faces before her.

A yellow lab came around the counter and sat, curling her tail around her legs. She looked up at Calvin.

"You have a dog in here?" Calvin cried.

"That's Molly. She's a local celebrity." Isabel handed him his change with a smile. "That'll be right up for you."

Calvin glared at the dog. "That's so unsanitary," he mumbled, wandering toward a display of baked goods.

"Can you please explain to me why I want a dynamite?"

"Because no self-respecting Mainer should go her whole life without a dynamite. That's why. Think of it as another attempt on my part to civilize you."

Gertrude curled her upper lip. "You're a cranky old man."

"Who just bought you lunch."

Gertrude couldn't think of a retort for that. So she stared longingly at the drink cooler, where a whole row of Yoo-hoos were calling to her. She knew she could dig through her walker pouch for some spare change, but she didn't think she had enough and didn't want to get her hopes up.

"Dynamites!" Isabel called enthusiastically, and Calvin and Gertrude headed back to the counter.

"Thank you," Calvin said, taking one of the cardboard dishes from the counter.

"Forks and napkins are right there," Isabel said, pointing. Then she looked at Gertrude. "Why were you asking about the curse?"

"The curse?"

"Yeah. You said the haunting."

"Oh, I didn't know it was a curse."

Calvin set his lunch back down on the counter.

Isabel leaned over the counter. "Yeah, the story goes that Tallia Bachman cursed the lake when she was drowning in it." She leaned even closer and lowered her voice. "She was the owner's daughter."

Gertrude leaned closer to Isabel and whispered loudly, "Someone owns the lake?"

Isabel stood up quickly, reestablishing the buffer between customer and customer service. "No, The Happy Trout. The owner of *this* place."

"Oh," Gertrude said, a little disappointed. "Where is this Happy Shark owner anyway?"

Isabel furrowed her brow in confusion, but then apparently decided not to bother with a correction, and looked toward the back, where a set of large double doors opened onto an expansive deck. "Last I knew, he was out with the boats, but I'm not sure if he still is. I wouldn't say anything to him about it though."

"Oh, I wouldn't," Gertrude lied. "So, this ghost—anybody seen her lately?"

"Seen? No. But we've heard her. Scared the heck out of me the other night. Screaming, but it sounded far away, like it was coming from the *middle* of the lake. Others have heard her too. Two of the cottages beside us have sold their properties in the last month. Those people say it was just a coincidence, that their sales have nothing to do with the curse, but no one believes them."

"What two cottages?" Calvin asked.

She pointed to the wall to her right. "The one right next to us. That was owned by some rich people from Massachusetts"—Calvin grunted self-righteously—"and then the next one is still owned by a local. Carlotta's been there for a hundred years—"

"Carlotta?" Calvin interrupted, his voice a higher pitch than usual.

"Yes, Carlotta, and then the next cottage, also owned by people from away, they sold too. So it's just us and Carlotta left here in this piece along the road, but now we're going to sell too." She didn't sound too upset about this impending job loss.

"What's Carlotta's last name?" Calvin asked.

"I don't know," Isabel said.

"Why do we care?" Gertrude asked.

"I knew a Carlotta once," Calvin said whimsically.

Gertrude scowled at him. Then she looked at Isabel. "So who's buying all these properties?"

"Some outfit from out of state. Vacationland Development."

4

"I *told you* Vacationland Development was suspicious!" Gertrude exclaimed. Calvin and she were on the deck attached to the back of The Happy Trout, in the bright sunshine, and Gertrude was trying to determine the easiest way to sit at the picnic table. She'd gotten stuck in one of those more than once and didn't want to do it again.

"They're still just buying properties, Gertrude. That's what real estate companies do," Calvin said.

Gertrude opted to just straddle the bench and sit sideways to the table. She picked up her plastic fork and looked down at the concoction on her plate. "What is this stuff?"

"Dynamites." Calvin shoved a giant forkful into his mouth.

"I know that. But what's in it? Looks like an awful lot of vegetables." In her paper basket sat an open hot dog bun and a pile of runny tomato-based goo with big chunks of green pepper and onion poking out. "And no cheese."

"Just eat it," Calvin said, and took another bite.

Gertrude gingerly took a bite and then regretted it. She quickly grabbed her glass of tap water and gulped it down.

"Got some kick to it, doesn't it?" Calvin said proudly.

Gertrude gasped for air. "It tastes like fire," she said, her voice raspy and her eyes watering.

"I know," Calvin said, his eyes full of unabashed joy.

Gertrude pushed the lunch away from her and looked around the deck. "You think he's out here?"

"Who, the owner?"

"Yeah."

"I don't know. Does it matter? We're not going to question him about his ghost daughter. Even you've got more class than that."

A small motorboat was docking in a slip on the far end of the dock. The man on the boat threw a line to a boy on the dock. The boy missed the catch, and an older man started hollering at him for doing so, while he bent over the water and fished around for the line.

When he finally got a hold of it, and stood back up, he found himself looking down at Gertrude. "Can I help you?" he asked, obviously annoyed at her proximity. He stepped around her and bent to wrap the line around a cleat on the dock.

"Are you the owner of Silly Shark?"

He stood and looked at her. "What?"

She thought it had been a simple enough question, but she decided to move on. "Why are you selling to Vacationland Development?"

"Who are you?"

"Gertrude, Gumshoe."

"Gumshoe?" He laughed. "Surely that's not your actual name."

"No. It's my calling."

He blinked, surprised. "I'm an old man, Gertrude, Gumshoe. They made a generous offer. I'd be a fool not to take it."

"What can you tell me about Tallia?"

His face darkened. "If you'll excuse me, I have work to do." He stepped around her and walked away. She started to give chase, but Calvin beckoned to her from their picnic table, so she headed that way instead.

"Looks like that went about as well as I expected," he said when she got close.

She looked at the trash on the table. "You ate *both* dynamites?"

He nodded proudly.

"Aren't you going to get heartburn?"

He shrugged and stood up. "Some things are worth the aftermath." He picked up his trash. "Let's go."

"Where are we going?" She followed him to the trash can.

"Let's go see Carlotta. I think I know who she is. How many Carlottas can there be in central Maine?"

Even though Carlotta's cottage was only two doors down, they had to walk back out to the road. The properties, though closely arranged, were separated by fences that extended out into the lake, making a cross-country jaunt or a stroll by the water impossible.

So they made the short walk down the road and then down the driveway to Carlotta's door. Calvin rang the doorbell, his hand trembling.

"You nervous? Or are the dynamites giving you a case of the shakes?"

Calvin ignored her. The door opened. "Carlotta?" Calvin's voice was full of hopeful wonder.

The woman hesitated, squinting at the man at the door. "Calvin? Is that you?" Her face blossomed into a wide smile. "Calvin!" She flung the door open and threw an arm around his shoulder.

Gertrude felt something akin to rage rise up in her. It seemed to come from the tips of her toes, and when Carlotta planted a kiss on Calvin's cheek, she thought it might explode out the top of her head. "I'm Gertrude," she said, trying to step between them. There wasn't room, of course, and this just made for an awkward collision between her walker and the open metal screen door.

"Yes," Calvin said, seeming to come back to himself. "Carlotta, this is my good friend, Gertrude. Gertrude, this is my old friend, Carlotta."

"You watch who you're calling old there, Buster!" Carlotta said, her voice full of charm and grace.

Gertrude couldn't stand the sound of it. "We're here on business."

"Business!" Carlotta said as if Gertrude said they were there to deliver cotton candy. "Well then, come right in!" She opened the door wider and stepped back to make room for them. "Can I get you some iced tea?"

"Do you have Crystal Light?" Gertrude asked, walking through the doorway and into the cottage, which looked like a *Murder, She Wrote* set.

"I do!" Carlotta said, her voice dripping with a graciousness that was driving Gertrude crazy. "Would you like lemon or grapefruit?"

"I'll take tea," Gertrude said through gritted teeth.

Calvin gave her a dirty look, but Carlotta didn't even seem to notice. "Sugar and lemon?"

Afraid of further angering Calvin, Gertrude just said, "Sure."

"Have a seat in the sitting room," Carlotta said. "I'll go get the tea."

Gertrude followed Calvin into a living room that featured a giant bay window that looked out on the lake. Calvin's breath caught. "This is beautiful."

Gertrude had never wanted to leave anywhere so badly in her life. "It's all right. If you like this sort of thing." She sat down and looked around the room for something to criticize.

Carlotta joined them with a tray of iced tea, which she gracefully set down on a polished coffee table. Gertrude was overcome with a desire to catch this woman in a crime. Carlotta handed Gertrude a glass of tea with a smile. Gertrude accepted the glass without one. She took a sip. It was delicious. Even the iced tea was perfect.

"So," she said, as Carlotta settled into a chair, "how do you and Calvin know each other?"

"We went to school together," Carlotta cooed. "Calvin here was the big basketball star. I was a cheerleader."

Calvin blushed.

Gertrude thought she was going to be sick. "And have you seen each other since?"

Carlotta looked sad. "I don't think so. Have we, Calvin? Maybe a few times after graduation, but not for years and years. You know, people go their separate ways, get married, spend decades chasing their children around. Are you still in Mattwooptock, Calvin?"

He nodded. "I sold the house though, and bought a trailer. Wanted to make sure I had the finances for a nice long, peaceful retirement."

"Oh, how lovely for you!"

Gertrude rubbed her temple, where a dull throb had taken root.

Carlotta looked around her cottage. "This place is more than I can afford really, but I just can't give it up. I have sixteen grandchildren ..." She paused to allow for reaction.

Gertrude didn't give one.

"Sixteen?" Calvin cried. "Holy smokes!"

Carlotta tittered. "I made babies who love to make babies. I had five children. They don't all live around here, but they *all* come back in the summer. The kids just love this place, so I just can't see leaving. I'll stay here till they take me out on a stretcher." She gazed out the window, and then added, "My Fred passed on five years ago now."

There was an awkward silence.

"My wife died ten years ago," Calvin said quietly.

"I'm so sorry," Carlotta said softly. Then she slapped her lap with both hands. "But, enough sadness! What business brings you here today?"

"We're investigating the curse," Gertrude said, too loudly, so glad that the conversation had moved on.

"The Clearwater Curse?" Carlotta raised her eyebrows. "Why on earth are you looking into that?"

"We heard people had heard screaming."

"Oh, that's just foolishness. I've lived here forever, and I've never heard anything." She looked out the window.

"Psst," Gertrude whispered.

Carlotta's head snapped around to look at her. "What?"

Gertrude was disappointed. "I was just testing your hearing."

For the first time, Carlotta looked offended. "My hearing is sharp as a tack."

"Did you live here when the Bachman girl died?" Calvin asked.

"Oh yes, that poor dear." Carlotta smoothed out her perfectly-ironed slacks. "No one really knows what happened. She just vanished. Eli—that's her father, the owner of The Happy Trout—he found her canoe upside down in the lake, and her flip-flops floating nearby, like they'd been in the boat, or even on her feet, but she'd just vanished."

Gertrude scowled. "They never found the body?"

Carlotta shook her head. "They weren't too anxious to look, if I remember clearly. Tallia was kind of a troublemaker, and so when she went missing, the police said she'd probably just taken off. They certainly didn't dive into the lake looking for her. But Eli was certain that she'd drowned."

Gertrude thoughtfully analyzed what she'd just heard. "But if they never found the body, we don't even know if she's really dead?"

Carlotta looked at her as if she were dense. "I can't imagine where she's been all these years. No use having false hope. I'm sure she's with the angels."

Gertrude rolled her eyes. "What do you mean she was a troublemaker?"

"Oh you know, just how some teenagers act out. She fell in with the wrong crowd, had a boyfriend with tattoos, kept stealing from her father's store, but nothing serious. I do think she liked the wine, but she wasn't a criminal or anything."

Gertrude was fascinated. "So where does the story of the curse come from?"

Carlotta waved a hand. "Foolishness really. In the years that followed, teenagers would dare each other to take a boat out at night, said Tally was haunting the lake, but I don't remember hearing about any screaming until lately."

"That's bizarre," Calvin said, rubbing his chin. "People are just hearing random screaming in the middle of the night? How do we know some real live woman isn't being assaulted and is shouting for help?"

"They say the screams come from the water. People all around the shore can hear it. So if people on both sides of the lake say the sound comes from the middle of the lake, it probably does."

"But isn't that impossible?" Calvin said.

Carlotta shrugged. "Like I said, I don't pay much attention."

"What do you know about Vacationland Development?" Gertrude asked.

"Vacationland Development is an obnoxious company that is trying to buy the whole lake." Carlotta's perpetual pleasantness was replaced with wrath at the mere thought of Vacationland.

"Have they tried to buy your property?" Calvin asked.

"Over and over," Carlotta said. "It's bordering on harassment. I've told them again and again I won't sell, no matter what they offer, but they just don't stop. Their current offer is obscene."

Gertrude wanted to ask what the current offer was, but Calvin spoke before she could. "If Vacationland is buying properties on either side of you, then it would make sense they would really want yours."

Carlotta pursed her lips. "Well, too bad. They can't have it. They want to turn this whole stretch into a resort. Going to level it and start over. Well, they're *not* going to level my home! Eli was the last to fall. I don't know what finally made him agree to sell. They probably gave him a huge offer too, but I still can't believe he's going to let them have what he's spent his whole life building. Can you imagine tearing down The Happy Trout?" She looked horrified.

"He said he wanted to retire," Gertrude said.

"I suppose that's possible. But still. He's a stubborn old man. I didn't think he'd sell."

Gertrude looked at Calvin. "I think we should go back and talk to him."

"No," Calvin said.

"About what?" Carlotta said.

"About the haunting," Gertrude said, annoyed that she had to explain something so obvious.

"Oh, don't do that to him," Carlotta said. "There *is* no haunting, and he's been through enough. He was a miserable man *before* his daughter died, but since then, he's hardly even been human."

"What?" Gertrude said. "Why was he miserable before?"

"He has just always been a generally unhappy fellow. His wife died a few years before Tally did. He was very old-fashioned. Conservative and strict, but the tougher he got with Tally, the more she acted out. She was his whole world, and she couldn't stand him."

5

As soon as Gertrude got home, she called Andrea. "We've got a case. Come pick me up."

"What about Calvin?"

"What about him? I need to question someone. He doesn't want to. So I'm taking you as my assistant instead."

"OK!" Andrea sounded beyond excited. "I'll be there in a jiffy."

Despite Andrea's promise of speed, Gertrude could barely stand the wait. She stood there staring out the window waiting for Andrea to pull up. But that drove her nuts, so she went outside to sit on her steps and wait. But then that wasn't good enough, so she walked down the street and waited on the edge of the road.

Finally, Andrea pulled alongside her, rolling her window down as her Subaru came to a stop. "I told you I'd come get you. Why are you hitchhiking?"

Gertrude giggled. "I'm not hitchhiking, you nut." She shoved her walker in the back, and then fell into the front seat still smiling. She liked the idea that Andrea thought she was wild enough to hitchhike.

"So what's the case?"

"We're going after Vacationland Development."

Andrea groaned. "Not again."

"No, this time they're really up to something. So a long time ago, a girl by the name of Tallia ... or Tally ... disappeared. Everybody thinks she drowned in the lake. I'm not so sure—"

"What? What does that mean?"

"They never found a body. Anyway, apparently she cursed the lake or something before she died—"

"You just said she didn't die."

"Will you stop interrupting? I don't give a hoot about some stupid curse. Here's what I know. A girl's missing, and a shady real estate company is involved."

Andrea laughed. "You can't think Vacationland had something to do with something that happened years ago."

"I don't know yet. That's what I'm going to find out."

"And why didn't Calvin want to go this time?"

"Because we're going to talk to Tallia's father again, and Calvin doesn't think that's appropriate." She said the last word as if it tasted sour.

"Of course it's not appropriate! Why do I always have to go with you when you interrogate the grieving parents?"

As they argued, Gertrude gave Andrea directions, and soon they were lost. Andrea pulled over to the side of the road that had suddenly turned to dirt. "Turn on your GPS."

"Fine." Gertrude rolled over and reached into the back for her phone, which was in her walker pouch. Then she stabbed at the small screen with her stubby finger. "It says there's no such place."

"What did you type in?" she asked, looking out her windshield as if expecting a ghost to pop out of the woods.

"Silly Shark."

"How far does this curse extend? This place is giving me the shivers. What is Silly Shark?"

"It's the store that Eli owns."

"Give me that." Andrea yanked the phone out of Gertrude's hand and did a search. A few seconds later—"You mean Happy Trout?"

"Yeah! That's it!"

Andrea turned the car around and headed east.

Finally, they were circling the busy area looking for parking. "Popular spot," Andrea remarked.

"You can just drop me off at the door and then go park."

"No way. Then you'll start without me."

Andrea finally managed to wedge her Subaru between an ancient, rusty fourteen-passenger van and a porta potty.

When Gertrude opened her door, it smacked into the outhouse. "I don't know if I'm going to fit, Andrea."

"Suck it in," Andrea said without sympathy.

Gertrude did suck it in and managed to squeeze out through the gap, holding her nose the whole time. "That is one stinky throne," she said, her voice sounding nasally.

"Stop your complaining. We've got a long walk ahead of us." She was already fifty feet ahead of Gertrude.

"I'm not the one who parked in the boondocks!" Gertrude cried, hurrying to catch up.

Gertrude glanced up at the trout as they entered, surprised it was still hanging on. Eli was behind the counter now. Isabel was nowhere in sight. Eli's face did not exactly light up at the sight of Gertrude. She hurried to the counter before he could get away. "Just a few more questions for you. When did your daughter disappear?"

Eli leaned on the counter with his elbows locked. "Nineteen-ninety-five. Why?" His tone was cold and distant.

"And what makes you so sure she's really dead?"

Andrea elbowed Gertrude in the side—hard. It hurt, but Gertrude tried to ignore both the pain and her assistant.

"A father knows these things."

"Can you tell us what happened exactly?"

"Why?" he repeated.

"So that I'll stop asking," Gertrude said matter-of-factly.

Eli appeared to consider this for a while. Then he said, "There isn't much to tell. I couldn't find her one summer morning, and then I found the canoe later that day. She used to go out on the water sometimes at night, drink beer with her boyfriend. I figure that's what happened."

"Who was her boyfriend?"

"A good-for-nothing thug by the name of Tyson Ross."

"Did the police question him?"

"The police didn't question anyone. They didn't care about Tally. Said she probably ran off. Said there was no sign of foul play."

"But you don't believe that."

"She wouldn't have run off without Tyson, and he was around for days after, moping about, looking for her. I finally had to tell him to get lost. Which is what I'm about to tell you. No need digging up all this pain. It was years ago." He turned and walked away.

Gertrude scanned her brain, but she couldn't think of anything else to ask him. She looked at Andrea.

"Is that it?" Andrea asked.

Gertrude shrugged. "I guess so."

"We drove all the way out here for that?"

"I was hoping he'd say more." Gertrude headed toward the door.

"Oh sure," Andrea followed. "Why wouldn't he want to share his personal grief with a complete stranger?"

6

Andrea dropped Gertrude off in front of her door, but Gertrude went straight to Calvin's trailer. She pounded on the door and then let herself in. "I need your computer," she said as she walked by him. He was sitting in his recliner, watching television, and eating what looked like meatloaf, carrots, and cranberry sauce out of a tray.

He wiped his mouth with a paper towel. "I think I need to return to the habit of keeping that door locked."

"Why is it unlocked?"

"I thought you'd be over. Didn't want to have to get up. But I also thought you'd wait until I invited you in, not just charge in like a bull in a china shop."

She sat down at the computer. "Don't worry. You won't even know I'm here. I'll be quiet as a louse."

Calvin snickered. "I think you mean mouse, and I doubt it. So did you go back and see Eli?"

"How did you know?"

"Doesn't take a genius. What did he say?"

"That Tally had a boyfriend named Tyson Ross."

"That's it?"

"Pretty much." She tapped "Tyson Ross" into the search engine.

"And was Eli happy to see you?"

"Happy as a chickadee in June."

Her search returned thirteen million results. *Uh-oh*. The first several pages were dedicated solely to Tyson Ross the professional baseball player. She didn't think that was her guy.

Though that would make the case more exciting, he was far too young to have been dating an eighteen-year-old in 1995.

The results that followed were for either "Tyson" or "Ross," and stopped being for both. "Oh beans!" she cried out in frustration, and Calvin jumped in his chair.

"What's wrong?" he asked without turning around.

"Nothing. Just go back to your *Bonanza*." She typed Tallia Bachman into the unhelpful box, found a teenage poet in New Jersey by that name, and then came up empty. She tried Tally Bachman, and found a used car salesman in New Mexico. On a whim, she tried Tallia Ross. Maybe she had married her good-for-nothing thug boyfriend, but if she had, the Internet didn't know about it. Tally Ross was on Facebook, but she was only thirteen. Gertrude slid her chair back and cried, "Nothing!"

"Nothing what?"

"Your computer knows nothing."

"Good then. Maybe you could get your own."

This gave her another idea. She rolled back to the keyboard and typed in Vacationland Development. "Wowsa!" There were more than forty thousand results. Gertrude started clicking and reading. Within the last year, Vacationland had bought up multiple properties from Fort Kent to Lubec to Kittery. It seemed they had a presence in every county—even Somerset, where no one ever bought anything. Condos in Mattawooptock. A timeshare in Ogunquit. A luxury resort in Belfast. And the list went on.

She visited their website, which was enormous. Page after page. It would take her hours to read through the whole thing, and she quickly decided she wasn't going to do that. But even without reading the details, she could see that this company, which was headquartered in Massachusetts, seemed to have their fingers in lots of pies.

"Calvin, these fellas are huge."

"What fellas?"

"Vacationland. They are all over the place. Must have quite a boodle behind them."

"A boodle?"

"You know, cold hard cash. They must be *loaded*."

"Well, if they build things like condominiums, and then sell them, they probably make a lot of money. And I'm pretty sure those waterpark resorts make a killing too."

"But Mainers can't afford to go to those places."

"Mainers don't go to these places. I told you—summer folk do. They're not called *Work*land Developers. They're called *Vacation*land for a reason. They build resorts. People come from Boston so that Mainers can wait on them."

She gave up and shut the computer down. "You may have a point. Well, enjoy your microwaved supper. I've got to go feed the cats." She stood to go.

"Did you eat yet?"

She looked down at him, surprised. "I have not."

"There's another meatloaf in the freezer. If you're hungry."

Gertrude *was* hungry. "Meatloaf sounds downright yummy, Calvin. Thank you." So she microwaved herself a TV dinner, and then sat down on the couch to eat and to watch *Bonanza* with her favorite human. The cats could wait.

7

The next morning, it was Calvin's turn to knock on Gertrude's door, and he actually waited for her to answer it.

"Good morning," Gertrude said, her voice full of glee.

"Carlotta just called me—"

"Oh," Gertrude said, with no glee at all. "Come on in."

"Don't be grouchy. I think you'll like this." He stepped inside and shut the door behind him. "I mean, it's not exactly good news, but it's still news you'll like. She heard something last night."

"The screaming?"

"No. She heard *singing* outside her window. She is terrified. I told her we'd be right over."

"Is she going to call the police? I don't want to run into my good buddy Deputy Hale."

"She said she didn't want to call the police. She's worried they'll think she's crazy. She thinks she might be crazy. I can guarantee she's not. So hurry up! Get dressed!"

Gertrude looked down at her housecoat, and realizing that she wasn't dressed yet, was slightly embarrassed. She cleared her throat. "Be right back."

She rushed to get dressed and ended up putting on mismatched socks. One reached all the way to her knee and the other only her ankle. But she didn't want to take the time to change them. She didn't think Calvin would notice.

They pulled into Carlotta's driveway forty-five minutes later. Calvin knocked on the door—a little too enthusiastically, Gertrude thought. Carlotta answered within seconds and held the door open for them. She looked as though she hadn't slept in weeks. As Gertrude walked by her and into the quaint cottage, she noticed Carlotta staring at her socks. Gertrude pursed her lips and glared at the woman, but Carlotta didn't seem to notice.

"Come right in," she cooed. "I'm so glad you're here. Would you like coffee? I just made a fresh pot."

"Cream and extra, extra sugar," Gertrude said and went into the living room. She plopped down on the sofa and then realized Calvin hadn't followed her. He had followed Carlotta into the kitchen. Gertrude started to sulk.

She didn't thank Carlotta when she handed her a steaming cup of fresh coffee. She took a sip, and it had the perfect amount of sugar. She didn't want it to, but this cheered her up a bit.

"So tell me about this singing," Gertrude said.

What color was in Carlotta's cheeks faded. "Oh, it was just dreadful. I was sound asleep in bed, and it woke me up. It sounded as though it was coming from just outside my bedroom window. Now how would the ghost know which window to sing through? That just spooks me!"

"There is no ghost," Gertrude said. "Continue."

"Well, I didn't dare get up to look out the window. I just pulled the covers over my head and waited for it to stop. Which it did. For a while. Then just as I was starting to think it was all a dream, it started up again. I thought about calling the police. But what if it really was a ghost? They would think I was mad!"

"What song?" Gertrude asked.

"What?" Carlotta appeared flustered.

"You said the prankster was singing. What song was she singing?"

"Oh!" Carlotta put a hand to her chest. "It didn't make any sense. I could only hear bits and pieces. Something about Romeo bleeding. Who says such a thing?"

Gertrude waited for her to continue. "That's it? That's all you heard?"

"No, there was more. Let me think." She scrunched her face up like a concentrating toddler. "I know I heard the word 'drowning.' That's what gave me such a fright, and there was also something about paying the price ... and she kept saying the word 'always.'"

"Always?"

"Yes, I couldn't help but think she was saying she would always haunt me."

"I'm sure that's not what she was saying," Calvin said.

"Hang on. Let me get out my jitterbug." Gertrude pawed through her walker pouch for her cell. When she found it, she typed "Romeo bleeding" into the search box. "There's a movie called *Romeo Is Bleeding*!" Gertrude said with triumph. "Maybe you heard the theme song. Hang on." She navigated to the theme song, and the sound of a haunting saxophone filled the room.

"That's enough to give me nightmares," Carlotta said, "but it has no words, and the tune's not right."

"Well, I didn't know it was going to be a saxophone solo. Excuuuuse me!" She stabbed at the screen again. "There's also a documentary by that name. Oh! It's about a poet! I don't know if you know this, Carlotta, but I'm quite a poet myself."

Carlotta didn't look impressed.

Gertrude kept reading. "There's a soundtrack for this one too, but it looks like none of the songs are about Romeo. What else did you hear again?"

"Drowning," Carlotta said in a tone that suggested she herself was drowning.

"That's a little broad," Gertrude said.

"Sorry, I didn't take notes while I was under the blankets hiding for my life."

"Well, you should have!"

"Ladies!" Calvin said. "I don't think it matters what song it was. Gertrude, why don't you go look outside the window for footprints."

This suggestion annoyed Gertrude for many reasons. First of all, *she* was the gumshoe. *She* was the one supposed to be issuing orders. Second, why didn't she think of that? Third, she knew Calvin just wanted to be alone with his little rig. "Why don't you come with me, Calvin?"

Calvin looked at her, his eyes narrowed. "Sure. Let's go."

The sun was brilliant, its rays bouncing off the water, and they could hear the joyful screams of children swimming off the docks behind Happy Trout. "Almost makes you want to go for a dip," Calvin said.

"No thanks," Gertrude mumbled. They turned a corner. "There it is." She pointed to the window.

"What lovely marigolds!" Calvin exclaimed.

"If you're into that sort of thing." Gertrude looked down at the bed of flowers that ran along the side of Carlotta's house. "Calvin, look!" Most of the marigolds beneath Carlotta's bedroom window had been trampled on. A few were even broken off.

"Not a very graceful ghost," Calvin said.

"Nor a smart one. If you're going to fake being a ghost, tread lightly. It looks like the nincompoop got down on all fours here." She squatted down to take a look. "Oh Mylanta, there's actually a handprint here." The soil showed distinct impressions of five fingertips. "This is no ghost, Calvin."

"I can see that." Calvin stood up. "But it almost makes it more disturbing. What kind of human being does such a thing?"

Gertrude stood too. "I don't know, but I'm going to catch the son of a gun."

Calvin chuckled. "You actually look angry."

"I am angry. I don't appreciate it when some goon terrorizes an old lady."

Calvin's eyes widened. "I've never heard you call anyone old before."

"Oh, Carlotta is old all right," she said, heading back around the corner of the house. "*Much* older than myself."

8

Calvin and Gertrude decided to spend the night at Carlotta's. They would take turns standing watch, and explained to Carlotta that they had lots of experience with this sort of thing. Carlotta didn't seem convinced, but she did seem delighted to have someone to cook for, and prepared them a giant meal: pineapple glazed ham, rosemary potatoes, fresh green beans from her garden, and chocolate torte for dessert.

She asked Gertrude if she would like to help, and Gertrude told her that she was too busy. Then she sat down in the living room and watched television. She nodded off and woke when Carlotta invited her to the dining room table.

Gertrude was exceedingly uncomfortable in her present circumstances. She looked up and down the table. "Must be nice to have time for all this cooking."

Carlotta either wasn't offended or hid it well. "Oh, I love to cook. It seems that all my grandkids eat these days is microwaved junk. So when they come over here, I like to make sure they get a nice, big, old-fashioned meal."

"It looks lovely," Calvin said, spooning some potatoes onto his plate.

Gertrude didn't want to admit it, but the food was delicious. She didn't think she'd ever had pineapple glazed ham before, at least not that she knew of, and she ate until she couldn't possibly eat any more. "You better take the first shift, Calvin. I need a nap."

"You just had one!" Calvin said.

"That was before this feast."

"I'm so glad you enjoyed it," Carlotta said, and Gertrude realized she'd accidentally praised the meal, and wished she could take it back.

"I'm wondering if we should call an exorcist," Carlotta said abruptly.

Gertrude let out a cackle. "An exorcist? Why, are you possessed by something?"

"Of course not!" Carlotta snapped, finally sounding offended. "An exorcist can exorcise spirits from places too, not just people."

"Carlotta," Calvin said softly, "there is no spirit. I talked Gertrude out of telling you what we found, because, frankly, I thought it more alarming than the idea of a ghost, but your prowler is very much human."

Carlotta gasped. "How do you know?"

"There is ample evidence that someone was kneeling in your flower bed."

Carlotta gasped again. "Did they hurt my marigolds?"

Gertrude snorted.

"Your flowers are fine," Calvin said. "They're just lovely."

Carlotta's expression softened into a smile that Gertrude found a bit creepy. "Do you remember the first time you gave me flowers, Calvin?"

Gertrude thought she was going to be sick.

"I do," Calvin said, smiling. "They were wildflowers. I picked them for you just before the spring formal."

Carlotta tipped her head to one side and gazed at Calvin.

Gertrude wanted to smack her. "So who do you know who would want to try to scare you to death?"

The smile faded. "No one. I'm just a kind old lady who minds my own business."

See? She even calls herself old.

"Maybe just some teenager trying to pull a prank? But I still don't know why they would pick me." Carlotta stood and started to clear away the plates.

"I'll do the dishes," Calvin said. "You ladies go relax."

Gertrude followed Carlotta into the living room, and they settled in to watch the evening news. By the time Calvin joined them, the television had moved on to *Wheel of Fortune*.

"Kalamazoo and Saginaw!" Calvin cried out.

Gertrude jumped. "What? What language was that?"

"Very impressive, Calvin," Carlotta said. "You always were a clever one."

Gertrude sighed heavily.

After the game show, they found a rerun of *Matlock*. Trying to show off, Gertrude picked a character at random within the first five minutes of the show. "He's the bad guy!" Then she crossed her fingers for the rest of the episode. In the end, she was right, and Carlotta and Calvin praised her.

"I should go to bed now," she announced, thinking she should quit while she was ahead.

"You can have the guest room," Calvin said. "I'll take the first watch."

Gertrude stood, and then realized she was about to leave them alone together in the dark room, in the romantic blue glow of the television. She sat back down. "I'll take the first watch."

Calvin looked surprised. "All right. Then I'm going to go try to catch some Z's. Good night, Carlotta."

"Good night, Calvin." Her voice was syrupy.

"Make sure you lock your window," he said.

"I will." Carlotta watched him walk away and then said to Gertrude, "I guess I'll turn in too."

"All right then."

Carlotta toddled off, leaving Gertrude alone with the next episode of *Matlock*. She was tempted to watch it, but she wanted to be able to hear what was going on outside too. So she put the TV on mute, with subtitles, and then opened the living room windows just a crack. She settled back down on the couch and pulled a blanket up to her chin. Suddenly she missed her cats desperately. *What kind of a woman doesn't have a single cat?* She really didn't like Carlotta. She tried to guess the bad guy again, but got it wrong. *No one has to know.*

9

Shortly after midnight, just when Gertrude was fighting to stay awake, she heard it.

Screaming.

It was so faint, she could almost talk herself out of the fact that she had heard it. But then it came again. She leapt up and went to the window. She couldn't see anything. She shut the TV off and looked outside again, willing her eyes to adjust to the darkness. The moon lit up the lake, and lights glowed in houses across the water, but she didn't see any people or any supernatural beings. She heard it again. The hair on the back of her neck stood up. *There's no such thing as ghosts. There's no such thing as ghosts.*

She sensed a presence behind her and turned to look. Calvin stood only inches away. "Ahhhhh!" she screamed.

"Ah!" he shouted back.

"What are you doing?" she cried.

"Why are you screaming in my face, you crazy old bat?" He held onto his chest with one hand, and a chair with the other.

"You're not supposed to sneak up on a woman in the dark, especially one who is standing ghost watch!"

"I didn't sneak up on you! It's not my fault you're hard of hearing!"

"I am not hard of hearing!" Gertrude argued, taking care to enunciate every word.

The scream came again. Calvin took a step closer to the window. "What on earth is that? It really sounds as though it's coming from the water."

They stood where they were for another fifteen minutes, but the screams stopped coming.

"Well, I think I've done enough protecting for one night. You got the second half watch?"

Calvin looked at his watch. "I only slept for three hours. The next watch is going to be seven hours long?"

"Fine, wake me up in three." Gertrude lay down on the couch.

"Don't you want the guest room?"

"Nah, I don't want to miss anything."

Calvin sat in the recliner and turned the television back on—with volume.

"How are you going to hear anything with that thing blaring?" Gertrude mumbled into the couch cushion.

"Go to sleep."

Gertrude went to sleep.

Calvin tried to wake her up at three, but she grumbled at him to leave her alone, rolled over, and went back to sleep.

When she woke to morning sunlight, he was nowhere to be found. Carlotta was in the kitchen making breakfast.

She stood, stretched, and made her way toward the smell of coffee. "Where's Calvin?"

Carlotta smirked. "Good morning. I just got up, and you two gumshoes were sound asleep. Good thing I had you for protection."

Gertrude flinched at her calling Calvin a gumshoe, but she let it go. She wanted to go to the bathroom more than she wanted to stay and argue.

After she did her business, she returned to the kitchen to find Calvin sipping a cup of joe. "I could use some sauce myself."

Carlotta pushed a mug toward her. Gertrude took a sip. Perfectly creamy and sweet. "Thank you," she said, and Calvin's eyes widened in surprise. "So, anybody serenade you last night?"

"I really don't think so. I didn't fall asleep till the wee hours of the morning, and then when I did manage to doze off, I'm pretty sure it was a light sleep."

"I should probably go check the dirt outside your window again just in case," Gertrude said.

"Did you hear the screaming?" Calvin asked.

Carlotta raised a perfectly penciled brow. "What screaming?"

"Well, first something screamed in the lake. Then me and Calvin did some screaming in your living room."

Carlotta's eyes widened.

"I did not scream!" Calvin argued.

"So you didn't hear any of that?" Gertrude took another sip of her coffee.

Carlotta shook her head.

"Your nighttime caroler must have had some pipes on her." Gertrude stood up and headed toward the door. "I'm not done with that coffee," she called back as she left.

She walked the perimeter of the house, but there was nothing to see. No footprints, no handprints, no broken flowers. She paused and looked at Calvin's truck in the drive. *Oh beans, we should've parked that somewhere else. We probably scared the prowler off.*

Gertrude gazed out at the lake, which was already filling with activity. A few boats taking off and a few early morning swimmers. She hurried back inside.

"Calvin!" she called as the screen door banged shut behind her.

"What?"

"Let's go."

"Where?"

"We're going to take a boat ride."

"What? What boat?"

Hmm. Gertrude looked around the small kitchen as if a boat might appear.

"Where are you trying to go?" Carlotta asked.

"I want to go look at that float out in the middle of the lake."

"Why?" Carlotta and Calvin asked.

Gertrude ignored them. "Where can I get a boat?"

10

"I've got a paddleboat," Carlotta said. "It doesn't go fast, but you could get there if you both worked the pedals."

"Perfect," Gertrude said. "Let's go."

"I don't know, Gertrude."

"Just trust me." She looked at Carlotta. "Well? Where's the boat?"

Wordlessly, Carlotta walked to the door, still in her slippers and bathrobe. Gertrude and Calvin followed her outside and down to the water's edge, where a small paddleboat was tied off.

"Are you even going to fit in that?" Calvin asked, sounding completely serious.

Gertrude glared at him. The same thought had occurred to her, but now that he'd said it out loud, she was going to *make* herself fit.

"It's a kids' boat," Carlotta said, as Gertrude stepped into the boat. It wobbled beneath her. She quickly spun around and dropped herself right into the molded plastic seat.

"Ow!" she cried softly. It had hurt far more than she'd expected it to, and more than she wanted to admit. She had jammed her hips into the narrow space and now she wondered if they would need a truckload of Crisco to get her back out. "All aboard!" she cried, in an attempt to disguise her pain.

Calvin climbed in, more carefully and gracefully than she had.

Carlotta shook her head, either in amusement or horror, and threw the line to Calvin. They were underway. Sort of. Calvin began to move his pedals, and Gertrude was delighted to see they were just like bicycle pedals. She was worried this was going to be more complicated. They were growing closer to Carlotta.

"Back! Back, Calvin!"

"Well, you could pedal too, you know!"

She began to pedal, and then realized she was doing it wrong too, and reversed direction. Soon they were creeping away from shore, and Calvin was starting to breathe heavily.

"I need a break."

Gertrude kept paddling, not wanting to admit that her legs were also growing tired. They began to spin in a lazy circle.

"Stop!" Calvin said.

"No! We don't have all day! Soon the float will be covered in juvenile delinquents!"

Calvin snorted. "They're not delinquents, Gert. They're just kids."

"Well, they should have a summer job."

"Did you have a summer job when you were twelve?"

Gertrude chose not to answer that. "All right, break's over. Let's go."

Calvin took a deep breath and began to pedal again, and their course straightened out.

"Good job!" Carlotta called from shore.

Gertrude rolled her eyes and pedaled harder. She so wanted to be farther away from that woman.

"Easy does it!" Calvin said, breathing hard.

They had to stop several times, and they fought the whole way, but within forty minutes, they were within twenty feet of the float.

"Slow down!" Calvin said. "We're going to miss it."

"What?"

"You're pedaling too fast, and you're forcing us left. We're going to miss the float. Slow your pedaling down!"

Gertrude slowed, and their wide bow swung right.

"Now you're pedaling too slow!"

"Oh, will you make up your mind, old man?"

The bow swung left again, and it became clear they were going to miss the float by several feet. Without thinking about it first, Gertrude lunged to the side and reached for the float. She would've flown right out of the boat and into the water, but her hips were stuck. She got the fingertips of her right hand on the edge of the float and squeezed with all her might. This pulled the boat closer to the float, and she was able to get a good grip. She stopped moving altogether, and they both just sat there silently, trying to catch their breath.

Finally, Calvin said, "Nice move."

"Thank you." Gertrude looked at the float carefully. She saw nothing. She reached farther down the float and pulled the boat along, inspecting the edge and top of the float as she went. She did this along one side, and then pulled them around to the next side of the float. A kid approached the float and looked at them warily. Gertrude gave him a dirty look. *Don't even think about climbing on this thing until I'm done investigating.* She rounded another corner and began to inspect the third side of the float. Still nothing. Then the fourth. The kid was still treading water, waiting for them to go away. She pulled herself around and they were back where they started. She kept going.

Calvin, who had been quiet for several minutes said, "I think we've seen all there is to see."

"We're done when I say we're done. *I'm* the gumshoe, remember?" She pulled them ahead some more. And then some more. The kid got tired of waiting and swam away. "There!" Gertrude pointed. There was something stuck to the top of the raft.

"What? I don't see anything."

"You wouldn't." She pulled them closer and reached out to touch it. It was some sort of residue on top of the raft. She scraped some of it off, which was no easy task, and then sniffed it. "Duct tape," she said as though she'd solved the case.

"What does that have to do with anything?"

Gertrude looked at him. "Tell me one legitimate reason there would be duct tape on a float."

Calvin shrugged. "Someone put up birthday balloons?"

Gertrude growled. "Get me back to shore. I don't want to be in this boat with you anymore."

It took them forty-five minutes to pedal back. Carlotta was right where they'd left her, still in her bathrobe. Though she had found a lawn chair and had settled in comfortably for the wait. "That was quite a show," she called out when they got close to shore.

"I don't think it's over yet," Calvin called back.

11

Calvin threw the line back to Carlotta. She stomped on it and then slowly bent to pick it up. Gertrude impatiently drummed the gunwale with her fingertips. Eventually they were tied up. Calvin slowly pulled himself to his feet. "I'll get out first. Then I'll help you."

"I don't need help."

Calvin stood on legs so shaky that Gertrude actually worried about him. Carlotta reached out a hand, and Calvin quickly grabbed it. "Just give me a second." They just stood there, holding hands. "All right," Calvin said, and took one giant step out of the boat. His foot didn't quite reach the shore, and splashed in the water.

Carlotta gave him a yank. "Are you all right?"

"Certainly." Calvin stepped onto dry ground. "Just a wet foot." They both turned to look at Gertrude expectantly.

She grabbed the bow and pulled herself forward. Her buttocks didn't budge. Not yet worried, she put her hands on either side of her seat and pushed down in an effort to push herself up. No movement. Now she was concerned. "Uh, Calvin? I'm stuck." She waited ten seconds and then added, "Well, don't just stand there looking at me! Help me!"

"I will," Calvin said. "I'm just trying to come up with a plan."

Gertrude was worried he would think of the Crisco. She was also worried he would just tip the boat over and hope she'd fall out. "Can't you just pull me out?" Her voice rose to a panicky pitch.

Calvin put his wet foot back into the water and reached for her hand. She took it. He gave her a pathetic tug.

"Why don't you just throw me a wet noodle?"

Calvin sighed and put his dry foot in the water too. He took her other hand and pulled. She didn't budge, but the whole boat moved forward and knocked him backward. He staggered, but didn't fall. Looking both exasperated and determined, he climbed back onto the boat. Gertrude couldn't imagine what good that would do, but she didn't want to be critical. Calvin sat on the bow and used his hands to pick up his left leg, which he then threw over Gertrude's head. She would've jumped, but she couldn't move. He was now straddling Gertrude. He took both her hands in his and then put both his feet on the back of her seat, bracing himself. "Ready? On the count of three. One ... two"—he took a deep breath—"and three!" He pulled backward with what appeared to be all his might, and Gertrude felt her hips wrench free.

"Ahhh!" she cried as she fell forward, slamming Calvin's back into the bow. She was lying directly on top of him, her face only inches from his.

"I can't breathe," he wheezed.

Embarrassed, she used both her hands to push off his chest, hard and fast. This sent her flailing backward, so far off balance there was no hope of recovery. She tried to throw her weight to the side to avoid falling back into the prison of that molded seat, and this sent her shoulder-first into the water with a mighty splash.

The water was so much colder than she'd expected. She gasped at the shock of it, and got a mouthful of water and slimy pond weed. She gagged, flailing all her limbs. *Oh Mylanta, I'm going to drown. They'll say the ghost got me.* She looked around wildly, but couldn't see anything. *I can't swim, I can't swim, I can't swim.* She kicked her feet and thrashed her arms. Her head came above the surface, and she gasped for air, but then she sank again. *How deep is it here? I'm going to drown. God, please don't let me drown.* She kicked harder, and her right big toe smashed into something incredibly hard. *A rock! A rock! Thank you, Jesus!* Pain shot up her right leg. Still, she smashed her foot back down toward what she thought was a rock and pushed up. She burst out of the water like a submarine doing an emergency blow. Up, up she came, wobbling on that right leg for several seconds until she thought to put the left leg down too. When she did, she realized that "the rock" had actually been the ground. She pushed up with both legs and stood, realizing with some shame that for all her thrashing, she had never been in more than two feet of water. She tried to stand up straight, wobbled, fell over backward, and then came into a squat, where she rested with just her head sticking out of the water.

Calvin and Carlotta were both laughing. She wanted to holler at them, but she couldn't stop coughing. As she slowly caught her breath, she reached up and pulled some grass out of her mouth. Then she stood, and dragged her soggy self to shore.

When she got there, she collapsed on the green grass and looked up at the blue sky. "I'm going to need a change of clothes," she said in a raspy voice.

"I think I've got a bathrobe that might fit you. It was a gift, and it's too big for me. You can even take it home."

I hate her. I really hate her.

Twenty minutes later, Gertrude was on Carlotta's couch clutching a fresh cup of coffee. She wore nothing but her birthday suit and Carlotta's bathrobe, which barely made its way around her. She was remarkably uncomfortable, and covered herself in a blanket for added security. Carlotta was outside hanging Gertrude's clothes up to dry. Gertrude was embarrassed that all of Clearwater would be able to see her skivvies.

Calvin repeatedly asked her if she was all right.

"Why didn't you help me?"

"The water was only up to your shins! I figured eventually you'd figure that out."

"My toe is killing me."

Calvin crossed the room and then bent to take a look. "Wow, that's really swollen."

"That's the wrong toe." She moved the injured toe closer to his face.

He jerked backward but then said, with compassion, "That one is even more swollen. Do you want some ice?"

"No thanks. I'm still quite cold." She looked out the bay window. "I can't believe those kids like to swim in such cold water."

"It's a deep lake. Deep water is cold water. Maybe that's why they didn't look for a body—they thought they'd never find it."

"I really don't think there was a body."

"I know you don't, and I'm sorry, but I think you're wrong. People don't just vanish permanently unless they're dead."

"Who's dead?" Carlotta reentered the living room.

"Tallia Bachman."

"Oh, yes, poor dear."

"Oh beans," Gertrude said. "I bet my cats are starving. Calvin, would you get me my jitterbug?"

"Sure. You going to call your cats?"

She looked daggers at him as she took the phone from his hands. "No, wise guy. I'm calling Andrea."

Andrea answered on the first ring. "Where are you?" she snapped without a hello.

"We are at Clearwater—"

"What? Why? What have you learned?"

"Well, we've heard a ghost screaming in the night, we found evidence of a caroling prowler with no respect for marigolds, and I almost drowned—"

"What? I'll be right there."

"No, wait, that's not why I called you."

"What?" Andrea sounded furious.

"I need you to feed my cats."

After several seconds of silence, Andrea said, "Fine. I'll go feed your cats. Then I'm coming. Are you at Happy Trout?"

Gertrude gave her cat-care instructions and then driving directions. Then she hung up the phone. "She's coming," she said, though it was clear Calvin and Carlotta already knew that.

"Who is Andrea?"

"She's my other assistant. Don't worry, she doesn't eat much."

Carlotta announced she was going to go make a big batch of chicken noodle soup from scratch and left the room. Calvin immediately fell asleep in his chair. Gertrude gathered every pillow in the room and made a small tower of them on the end of the couch. Then she lay down and propped her foot up. She knew she didn't need sleep, but she thought she should get her throbbing toe up in the air. Twenty seconds later, she too was asleep.

12

"Holy mackerel! It's all purple!"

Gertrude woke to find Andrea staring at her toe. Feeling oddly violated, Gertrude quickly sat up and threw the blanket over her feet.

"Gert, I think that toe is broken."

"Did you feed my cats?"

"Yes, your cats are fine. So fill me in!" Andrea pushed Gertrude's pillow tower over and sat on the end of the couch.

Calvin went through the story, pausing occasionally to answer Andrea's questions, which were plentiful. She was especially inquisitive about the song lyrics.

"Are you sure she said 'drowning'?"

"I'm not sure of anything," Carlotta admitted.

"That's a spooky lyric," Andrea said.

"Romeo bleeding is pretty spooky too," Gertrude said.

Andrea's face lit up. "Wait! I think I know what it is!"

Gertrude waited. "Well, are you going to share with the rest of us?"

"She said Romeo and bleeding and always and drowning, right?"

"Yes," Carlotta said, nodding eagerly, "and lots about love too."

"Exactly!" Andrea nodded emphatically. "It was 'Always' by Bon Jovi." Then Andrea startled them all by belting out the ballad.

Carlotta, eyes wide, started nodding. "That was it! I mean, I couldn't hear the whole thing, but that certainly sounds like the tune."

Andrea stopped singing, and her face fell. "Guys, that song came out in 1995."

"So?" Carlotta said.

"So? Isn't that when Tallia disappeared?"

This silenced the group for a while. Finally Calvin broke the spell with some reason. "If someone wanted to make us think they were the ghost of someone who died in 1995, it would make sense that they would pick a song from 1995. This doesn't prove it's a ghost. I think it proves just the opposite."

"I don't know," Andrea said slowly. "It's pretty eerie. Why are you all so reluctant to think it could really be a ghost?"

Gertrude rolled her eyes. "Oh, I don't know—because there's no such thing as ghosts?"

"Says who?" Andrea said.

"Says anyone with a brain!"

"Lots of intelligent people believe in ghosts, Gertrude. Some have even seen them. If there's no such thing as ghosts, what have thousands of people seen? Or heard? Or even communicated with?"

Gertrude didn't know the answer to this and had grown tired of the conversation. "Andrea, Tallia Bachman isn't even dead. So her ghost is wherever she is, still attached to her body. End of story."

"You can't possibly know that, Gertrude. And everyone else in the world thinks she's dead, including"—she said pointedly—"her *spirit*."

"This argument is starting to frighten me," Carlotta announced. "I liked it better when we weren't dealing with the supernatural."

"We're not," Calvin reassured her. "Supernatural beings don't leave knee-prints in flower beds."

"Even so, do you think you could spend the night here again?"

"Absolutely," Calvin and Gertrude said in unison.

"Can I stay too?"

Carlotta smiled at Andrea. "The more the merrier."

"Great. Then let's get started! What do we do next?"

Gertrude scowled at her. "What do you mean?"

"I mean, where do we go? Whom do we question?" She rubbed her hands together. "I'm ready for action!"

Gertrude leaned back. "I'm not going anywhere. My toe is busted."

"Sorry, Andrea. My legs are made of jello," Calvin said.

After a sad pause, Carlotta said, "I feel fine, but I'm not much of a detective. I am, however, an excellent cook. Let's have lunch!"

Gertrude limped out to the dining room. She couldn't believe how much her toe hurt. "Do you have any pain medication?"

Carlotta tittered. "I'm seventy-five! Of course I have pain medication." She disappeared into a hallway but was back in seconds with a bottle of pills. "I'm sorry, I should have thought to offer you some sooner."

"That's all right. You've had a lot on your mind."

With gratitude she did not want to show, Gertrude swallowed the ibuprofen and then dug into her soup. She was dismayed to see Carlotta had also found the time to make corn muffins. *Probably those are from scratch too.* But her disgust didn't stop her from eating three of them. They were the most delicious corn muffins she'd ever had. They practically melted in her mouth.

The four ate in a weary silence and then sat there looking at one another, as if they'd said all there was to say.

"Anyone want to play cribbage?" Carlotta asked suddenly.

"If I can play while lying down on your couch." Gertrude had no idea how to play cribbage, but she didn't want to be left out.

13

Gertrude took the first watch that night, and Andrea refused to let her do it alone.

"You should really get some sleep before your shift," Gertrude tried.

"I can't. I'm too amped up. I feel just like Sherlock in *The Hound of the Baskervilles.*"

"Well, calm down. I've seen that episode, and it was far more exciting than this will be. The most that is going to happen is we're going to hear some fake screaming."

"I meant the book, and if there's nothing to see, why are you staring out the window?"

Gertrude hadn't taken her eyes off the float for nearly an hour. "Something was taped to that float."

"So? Why are you staring at it now?"

Could you be any more annoying? "What would you like me to look at?"

Andrea didn't answer her, and stayed silent for a remarkable three minutes before exclaiming, "Oh my gosh!"

"What? Did you see a gigantic hound?"

"No! Look!" Andrea pointed out the window.

Gertrude tore her eyes away from the float and looked in the direction Andrea was pointing. *Oh my gosh indeed.* It was hard to make out, as what they were looking at was so far away. "It's a person," Gertrude said, just to get that out there before Andrea started claiming the supernatural, "and it's ... she's ... *glowing.*"

"Sure, lots of *people* glow in the dark."

Gertrude didn't respond. She didn't know how to. It appeared the woman was wearing a white dress, though it could have been any light color. She wondered what Tallia was wearing when she disappeared.

"Oh beans! Where's my jitterbug?" She fumbled around in the dark until she found her phone, and then she fumbled some more to get the camera turned on. Then she zoomed in and videoed the figure as it walked.

She didn't think this was a ghost, but it sure looked like one, almost *floating* along the opposite shore. "I wish we were in a house on that side of the lake. They've got a great view. Come on, Andrea, let's get closer."

Gertrude stopped filming and turned to find her walker.

"What? Are you going to walk around the lake?"

"Don't be foolish. You're going to drive me."

"Gertrude, wait ... she's gone."

Gertrude returned to the window. There was nothing to see.

"She disappeared." Andrea's voice was full of wonder.

"Or she just stopped glowing. We wouldn't be able to see her then."

"Maybe." Andrea obviously didn't believe that for a second.

"Come on, we can still go have a look."

"No! I'm not driving you around in the dark to look for a ghost, and I'm certainly not going to sneak around through people's yards at midnight. What if someone calls the cops? Aren't you in enough trouble?"

"I didn't say anything about sneaking through yards."

"No, but you were thinking it."

Gertrude had no argument for that. Andrea obviously knew her better than she'd thought. "Fine." She pulled a chair over to the window and sat, focusing her eyes on the spot where she'd last seen the glowing person. Andrea sat behind her in a recliner and kept talking. She had an endless supply of ghost stories, most of them based in Maine, all of them, according to her, unarguably true. Halfway through a story about a haunted lighthouse, Gertrude accidentally nodded off.

An hour later Calvin woke her up by shaking her shoulder. She sat up straight. "I wasn't sleeping!" She noticed Andrea had fallen asleep in the chair.

"Shh ... look!" Calvin pointed out the window, just as Andrea had done.

Gertrude looked. Farther down the shoreline, the glowing human had reappeared.

"Do you see that?" Calvin asked.

"Of course I see it."

"Good. I thought I was losing my mind."

"Andrea and I saw it earlier too."

"And you didn't wake me up?"

Gertrude felt guilty. "Sorry. It all happened so fast. Want to go chase her?"

"Who? The ghost?"

"She's not a ghost, and yes, the woman who is glowing in the dark. Let's go after her."

Calvin didn't say anything.

"Come on, Calvin, before she stops glowing!"

Calvin didn't move.

"Calvin!" Gertrude almost hollered.

"I don't want to chase her," he said softly.

"Are you scared?" She couldn't believe it.

"No. I just don't want to chase her. I'm exhausted. And old. My legs are still killing me from the last adventure you dragged me out on."

"Chase whom?" Andrea squirmed in the chair behind them.

"Oh for heaven's sake, you two are no help."

"It doesn't matter now. She's gone," Calvin said.

"She's not *gone*, Calvin. People don't just vanish into thin air. She just stopped glowing."

"Either way. No point in going out there now."

"Fine, you big wimp. I'm going to bed. Wake me up if she lights up again." Gertrude stretched out on the couch and went back to sleep, and dreamt of a glow-in-the-dark Bon Jovi.

14

At breakfast the next morning, the three senior sleuths tripped over themselves to tell Carlotta what they'd seen. The more they talked, the more the color drained from her face, and the closer to the floor her lower jaw fell.

Gertrude showed her the video, which was less than impressive. All they could see was darkness, with a glowing orb bobbing along across the screen. "We need to get a better jitterbug next time."

"This can't be real," Carlotta said.

"It's not," Gertrude said. "Don't worry." She looked at Calvin. "You know what we need?"

"An EMF detector?"

Gertrude scowled. She didn't know what that was. "No, we need Dave."

Calvin sneered. "Why do we need him?"

"I bet he can find Tallia."

Calvin looked incensed. "First of all, you need to let it go, Gertrude. We're not going to find Tallia, because she probably can't be found, because she's probably dead. Second, what could Dave do? He's not a magician!"

"No, he's a spook. He's got connections. He can do things."

"Why? Because you've just decided that about him? In your little fantasy world? You don't even know the man."

"Why are you being so mean to me, Calvin?"

"Who is Dave?" Carlotta asked, breaking the tension.

"He's a spy," Gertrude said. "I think. I don't really know what he is. But I found him up north in a cabin full of guns when I rescued a bunch of old ladies from a crazy kidnapper." Carlotta's eyes grew wide, which encouraged Gertrude. "And then he rescued me when I was kidnapped by an arms dealer on the border."

Calvin stared at her. "What? Dave was part of that?"

"The Mexican border?" Carlotta asked.

Calvin scoffed. "No, the infamously dangerous Canadian border."

Gertrude scrunched up her face. "Well, it seemed pretty dangerous when that little criminal was poking a gun into my back."

"My!" Carlotta held a delicate hand to her chest. "You *do* have adventures!"

"Anyway, Dave rescued me then too. He just happened to be there. So I think he is some sort of crime fighter himself. Otherwise, why would he always be turning up where the action is?"

"Bad luck?" Andrea offered.

The room was quiet for a few minutes, and then Andrea asked, "So how do we find him?"

"Well, usually, I just go to northern Maine and try to get myself killed. Then he just appears. Beyond that, I have no idea how to get in touch with him."

"You don't know where he lives? Not even a town?" Andrea said.

Gertrude shook her head.

"Is he on social media?"

Gertrude laughed. "Of course not. He wants to be invisible. I don't even know his real name. I highly doubt it's Dave."

Andrea slapped her leg. "I've got it!" Everyone looked at her expectantly, and she seemed to glow in the spotlight. "When Sherlock needed to find someone, he'd put an ad in the paper."

"No one reads papers anymore," Calvin said dismissively.

"No," Gertrude said, "but *everyone* reads *Uncle Henry's*."

Carlotta didn't have a computer, so Gertrude had to use her phone. She navigated to "Create New Ad," and then looked at Andrea. "What do I write?"

"Isn't *Uncle Henry's* where people trade puppies and guns?" Carlotta asked with a critical tone Gertrude didn't appreciate.

"And everything else," Gertrude said. "You can find *anything* in Uncle Henry's. Even a job. Even a spouse."

Calvin barked out a laugh. "Who finds a spouse in a swap magazine?"

"It's been done," Gertrude said impassively. Then she looked at Andrea, waiting for instructions.

Andrea leaned forward and rested her elbows on her knees. "How about this. All caps: DAVE! We know who you are and we need your help. Give him your phone number and then say, 'Help us, and we won't tell anyone what we know.'"

"Good heavens," Calvin said, "that is going to attract all sorts of scary phone calls."

"All *Uncle Henry's* ads do," Gertrude said, and started typing. "I'm going to add, 'It's a matter of life and death' just for good measure."

"Perfect," Andrea said.

Gertrude hit "Post" and set the phone down. Then she just as quickly picked it back up and looked at the time. "Oh horsefeathers!"

"What?" Calvin cried.

"Calvin, you've got to get me to church, quick!"

"Change your mind about the exorcism?" Carlotta sounded hopeful.

"No! I'm supposed to start community service in a half-hour!"

Calvin looked horrified. "You didn't tell me that!"

"Well, I'm telling you now! Let's go!"

"You can't go like that. Your toe is broken, and you still have pond scum in your hair."

"It's a homeless shelter. I'll fit right in."

"Gertrude! That's so rude!" Andrea cried.

"I used to live there, so I can say whatever I want."

"Your church is a homeless shelter?" Carlotta looked so confused. "And you used to *live there*?"

Gertrude pointed at Andrea. "You watch her. Take care of her. Protect her. I'll be back before dark." Then she looked at Calvin. "Hustle!"

15

Gertrude dragged herself back through Carlotta's door at half past six.

"How did it go?" Carlotta chirped.

Gertrude grunted. "I did laundry for eight hours. How do you think it went?" She walked past Carlotta and into the living room.

"It could be worse," Calvin said, and Gertrude knew what he meant: at least she wasn't in jail.

Gertrude collapsed on the couch. "What did I miss?"

"Nothing," Andrea said, sounding sad. "No screams, no sightings—"

"No, I mean, what did I miss for food? Did you guys eat supper yet?"

"Of course not!" Carlotta sang out. "We've been waiting for you! We have pasta with homemade meatballs, and garlic bread."

Gertrude's belly growled in delight. As much as she disliked Carlotta, she was thinking of moving in permanently. "Carlotta!" she called. "How do you feel about cats?" She hobbled into the kitchen, leaning on her walker even more than usual, just in time to see Carlotta scowl.

"I am deathly allergic to them."

I knew she couldn't be trusted.

"I take it you haven't heard from Dave?" Carlotta said.

"No, not yet."

Andrea appeared beside her. "Did you feed your cats?"

"No, Calvin did while I was breaking rocks in the hot sun."

65

"That was awfully generous of him," Carlotta cooed.

"Well, that's what partners do," Gertrude said pointedly.

Carlotta invited everyone to the table, and they all sat down. Andrea was humming. Gertrude gave her a dirty look.

"Sorry, got that darn Bon Jovi song stuck in my head."

"Well, stop it. It's creepy." Gertrude put her napkin in her lap. She didn't usually do this, but she was trying to keep up with Carlotta's etiquette. "Andrea and Calvin, I'm going to need you two to stand watch tonight."

"Oh?" Calvin said. "You too tired from all the laundry?"

"No. I'm going to sleep outside, on the shoreline. Wait for the ghost."

Andrea dropped her fork, and it made a loud clank sound that made Gertrude jerk her head up. When she did, she saw her three companions staring at her.

"What?"

"I know you do crazy things in the name of crime fighting, Gert," Calvin said, "but that's just beyond crazy. I just ... you can't ... please don't do that."

"I'll be fine." She looked at Carlotta. "Do you have a sleeping bag I can borrow? I doubt I'll do much sleeping, but I don't want to catch a chill."

They all continued to stare at her, silently. No one was even chewing anymore. Gertrude couldn't imagine why they were so shocked. She'd wanted to go after the creepy glowing woman the night before—why wouldn't she want to tonight?

Finally, Carlotta swallowed hard and said, "Of course I have a sleeping bag. And you should have a tarp too, for under the sleeping bag. So you don't get too wet—again. And I'll get you a pillow." Carlotta slid back from the table.

"You can finish eating first, Carlotta," Calvin tried, but she ignored him.

Gertrude *did* finish eating. The ghost could wait. She was famished. She ate until there was no food left in sight. Then she looked down at the bag Carlotta had packed for her. "Thank you. You wouldn't happen to have any antacids I could take along?"

Carlotta wordlessly disappeared to fetch the chewables.

"Gertrude, are you sure about this?" Calvin asked.

"As sure as pumpkin pie in October."

"What time do you want to go?"

Gertrude looked at him, and then looked out the window. It wasn't quite dark yet. "We can head out anytime, but I don't want to set up camp until after dark. Don't want anyone to see me."

Calvin shook his head, and then slid his chair back. "All right, let's go."

"Wait!" Carlotta came back with antacids and a flashlight. "And here's my phone number, just in case you need anything."

Gertrude thanked her and followed Calvin outside.

He helped her into the truck, something he never did, and she looked at him in surprise.

"I thought your toe might get you into trouble."

She thanked him and watched him walk around to his side of the vehicle. He didn't look to be in too good a shape either. "You sure you don't want me to stay out there with you?" he asked after climbing in.

She couldn't remember having said that, but she thought maybe he was just *wishing* she'd said that, so she made it easy on him. "No, you get some rest. I'll be fine." He pulled out onto the main road and drove past The Happy Trout. The tar road curved away from the lake after that, but Calvin turned down a dirt road that circled the lake. Off this road sprang driveways and camp roads galore. "Just a little farther," Gertrude said. She had no idea where she was going, but was trying to guess the location she'd seen the glowing woman the night before.

"I think we've already gone by the area we saw her," Calvin said.

"All right. Drop me off then."

Calvin took the next drive, which split into three driveways, each of them leading to a small cottage on the water. At one of the cottages, a dozen people were gathered around a campfire, and even more were cheering on a horseshoe match lit by tiki torches. "Keep me away from that bunch!"

Calvin obliged, and followed the path to the camp farthest from the festivities. He parked behind a large tree, and then, the truck still running, got out to help Gertrude out. She felt a pang in her gut at the thought of him leaving. *I'll be all right. I'm a gumshoe.* She slid out of the truck, and he put her walker in front of her. She grabbed her bag, and then, after slinging it over the handle of her walker, began to walk away.

"Wait!" Calvin caught up to her and gave her a stiff hug. "Call if you change your mind, all right?"

"All right," she mumbled into his shoulder.

16

There was obviously no one home at the nearest camp, and Gertrude thought about breaking in, but decided she didn't want to risk further conflict with Deputy Hale. She couldn't catch a fake ghost if she was locked up in the clink. Instead, she crawled under the back deck of the camp and made herself a little nest. She spread out her tarp and only then thought to make sure she wasn't invading any other critter's territory. She shone the flashlight around the small space, but didn't see any eyeballs. Satisfied, she stretched out her sleeping bag and got comfortable. A few times she nodded off, but then jerked awake to watch the shoreline.

At about midnight, she heard a noise she really didn't want to hear. Raindrops. *Aw, well, I'm under cover at least*, she thought. But then the drops became streams, streams that fell from the sky and then flowed under the deck and over her tarp. By the time she felt it happening, it was far too late. Her backside soaked, she jumped up and rapped her head on the bottom of the deck. She let out a cry that could easily have been interpreted as a ghost call by her friends on the other side of the water. She looked around in a panic, suddenly sure she was going to drown. She climbed out from under the deck to get to her walker, which was already soaked. *If my jitterbug is broken, I'm going to* have *to break into this cabin, Hale or no Hale.*

But her jitterbug wasn't broken. She fumbled through her pockets for Carlotta's phone number, but when she found it, it was soaked through and unreadable. She squinted and tried to recall the number from memory. When she thought she had it, she dialed.

"Buzzard's Breath Saloon?"

"Ah!" Gertrude screamed in frustration—into the phone—and hung up.

She scrunched her face again, harder this time, got a vision of a similar number, and tried that.

It rang and rang, and then she heard the blessed sound of her beloved Carlotta. She would never think a bad thought about this beautiful woman again. "I need help," Gertrude said. "I'm drowning."

"Are you still where Calvin dropped you off?"

"What?" Gertrude had trouble hearing over the torrential downpour.

"Calvin told me where he left you," Carlotta said, too loudly. "Are you still in the same spot?"

"You don't have to holler. I'm not deaf. Yes, I'm still in the same spot, but not for long. I'm about to be washed away. Hurry!"

"I'll be right there." Carlotta hung up before Gertrude could clarify exactly *who* was coming to her rescue, but she decided she didn't care all that much.

She tried to shove all her bedding back into the bag, but it didn't quite fit anymore. She shoved her phone into her bra in a futile attempt to protect it from further saturation. Then she just leaned on her walker and waited, the rain pouring on her head and running into her eyes. If the fake ghost lady had been twenty feet in front of her, Gertrude wouldn't have seen her.

What seemed like at least five hours later, a car's headlights lit up Gertrude's backside. She spun around and then threw a hand up to protect her eyes from the blinding light. Then she moved, as fast as she could, at a speed that could hardly even be classified as movement, toward the light.

Carlotta came running toward her. "Oh you poor dear!" She tried to take the bag from Gertrude and instantly dropped it. "Oh my, isn't that heavy?" She dragged it toward the car, leaving Gertrude to continue her waterlogged trudge.

When Gertrude finally got to the car, Carlotta was trying to wrestle the bag into the trunk. It almost looked like she was trying to hide a body, and Gertrude let out a giggle. *I've been watching too much Hawaii 5-0*, she thought, and then squatted down to help Carlotta lift.

Carlotta slammed the trunk shut, and then they both scrambled into the car. Once safely inside, Gertrude realized she was trembling all over, and tried to take several deep breaths.

Carlotta turned the heat up. "Something about Clearwater—it just likes to keep you soaked."

"Yeah. I think I'm going to need to borrow your housecoat again ... Not that I'm not grateful, but why did you come? I figured you'd just send Calvin." Gertrude scanned the woods as they drove through them, looking for the pretend poltergeist.

"Oh, he was sound asleep. The phone was right beside the bed. I'm the one who answered it, so I figured, why don't I just go? Let the others sleep. Besides, I figure I owe you for all your help."

Gertrude smiled in the darkness.

"Speaking of Calvin," Carlotta continued.

Gertrude stopped smiling.

"I just wanted you to know that I have no romantic designs on him."

Gertrude coughed. "What? Why are you telling me that?"

Carlotta paused, and then said, "I think you know why."

"No, I *don't*." Gertrude spoke the last word with an unnatural and unnecessary emphasis.

"All right. I just wanted to put it out there. He's a wonderful man, but I am too old and too busy with my grandkids to get caught up in any whirlwind romance. Besides, I don't think I could compete with you."

Gertrude thought her heart might stop with shock.

"I mean, I can cook sure—but you, well, you really know how to have fun! Calvin wasn't this full of life when he was eighteen!" She let out a joyous cackle that was contagious.

Gertrude joined in her laugh, picturing an eighteen-year-old Calvin in front of the TV, watching *Bonanza* with his feet up.

17

"I take it you didn't see anything?" Andrea said, and Gertrude didn't like her tone. They were seated around the breakfast table, eating waffles—from scratch—with real butter and real maple syrup. Gertrude liked Carlotta's cooking even more now that she knew she wasn't doing it just to woo Calvin.

"Of course not. Hard to see anything when you're drowning."

Gertrude's cell rang. A Maine number showed up on her caller ID, but she didn't recognize it. "Hello?" she said, sounding suspicious.

"Gertrude?"

She instantly recognized that tightly controlled voice. "Dave!" She pointed to the phone and mouthed to her cohorts, "It's Dave!"

"We know!" Calvin mouthed back.

"Listen," Dave said, "we don't have much time. I'm going to give you an address. Write it down."

Gertrude waved her hand at Calvin, which was supposed to mean, "Get me a pen," but Calvin had no idea what it meant and told her as much with his blank stare.

"Pen! Now!"

Carlotta sprang into action.

"You need to get to that address as soon as you can," Dave said. "I'm assuming you're still in Maine?"

"Yep!"

"Good. Then get there. But this is the most important part. Before you do anything, take a hammer and smash your cell phone. Smash the snot out of it. Then make sure you pull the battery out—"

"Can't I just *take* the battery out?"

Carlotta returned with pen and paper.

"We don't have time for you to figure that out. Just smash it. Seconds matter, so stop arguing. Then get to this address. But be careful you're not followed. They're probably already watching you. You've got to lose them. If they follow you to this address, and find me, we'll have serious trouble." He gave her the address, and then said, "Now smash the phone. Now!" And he was gone.

Gertrude looked at the silent phone in her hands. She thought she might cry. "Carlotta, I'm going to need a hammer."

"Seriously?"

"Now! A hammer! It's a matter of life and death!"

"I have one downstairs."

Gertrude got up and followed her into the basement, where Carlotta handed her the puniest hammer Gertrude had ever seen. "I didn't know they made hammers this little. It's like a baby hammer! Stand back!" She got down on all fours, put the phone on the basement floor, brought the hammer up over her head with both hands, said, "Sorry, friend," and brought it down as hard as she could—and missed completely. "Ow!" she cried as the force of the impact traveled up her arms.

Calvin and Andrea were on the stairs. "What are you doing?" Calvin cried.

Gertrude decided to try it with one arm, and used her other for balance. She brought the hammer down again and there was a satisfying crack as the screen caved in. This was more fun than she'd expected. She did it again, and the phone splintered further.

"Gertrude! Have you lost your mind?"

Crash! Again. And again. The phone was a mess of fragments. Gertrude pulled them apart and found something that looked like a battery. She pulled it out and tossed it aside. Then she looked at Calvin. "All right. Let's go."

She headed up the stairs, pushing them ahead of her. "Dave says they're probably already outside watching us—"

"Who's watching us?" Calvin asked.

"Bad guys. We've got to make sure we're not followed. So everyone, keep your eyes peeled."

They spilled outside, and all of them looked around wildly. "There!" Gertrude cried. A black SUV was parked across the street. The windows were tinted, but it was facing them.

"Everybody in!" Calvin cried.

"Shotgun!" With one hand, Gertrude tossed her walker into the bed of the pickup, and then climbed in front.

Calvin backed out of the driveway and drove away. The black SUV didn't move. "False alarm," Calvin said, and everyone let out a collective breath. But a half-mile later, Calvin said, "Oh no." Gertrude turned around to look and sure enough, the SUV was two cars behind them.

"We've got another problem," Gertrude said, looking down at the address in her hands.

"What?" Calvin said.

"How are we going to find this place without my jitterbug's GPS?"

"We could use a map?" Andrea said.

"We don't have any *maps*," Calvin said, "because we've always had a GPS. What's the address?"

"Dead Water Road, Moscow."

"*Moscow?*" Carlotta cried. "That's an hour away!"

"Dead Water sounds ominous," Andrea said.

"It's worse than you think," Calvin said. "I think I know where he's sending us, and we're never going to make it with the men in black on our tail."

"Where are we going?" Gertrude asked.

"There's an old abandoned Air Force radar site up there. I can't imagine why he picked that spot, but I also can't think of anything else in Moscow. There's nothing else there. But let's not worry about that yet. First things first." Without slowing down, he jerked the pickup right onto a narrow dirt road, and accelerated. The move threw Gertrude into Calvin's lap. He gently pushed her back into her own seat. "Buckle up, Buttercup."

18

The four adventurers pounded over the rough road, leaving a giant cloud of dust in their wake. Gertrude reached up to grab hold of the handle over the door and yelled, "Yippee-ki-yay!"

Andrea was twisted in her seat, trying to look out the back window. "I can't tell if they followed us."

Calvin took another hard turn, this time left, and headed up a steep incline without slowing down.

"Calvin?" Carlotta said tentatively. "Do you know where you're going?"

"No idea."

Gertrude looked at him and beamed with pride. His hands were at ten and two, his knuckles white, his jaw firm. He was leaning forward as if that would help him see better. He looked so determined. So invested.

"They're never going to catch us," Gertrude said. "Don't worry, Carlotta." Gertrude looked out her window and down and saw that about a foot to her right was a drop-off so deep she couldn't see the bottom of it. She wasn't sure whether Calvin knew how literally they were living on the edge in that moment. "Hold 'er steady," she muttered.

Gertrude didn't breathe again until they had turned away from the cliff. Shortly after, they crested the top of the mountain and began their descent. Then Calvin slowed down for the first time. "Oh fiddlesticks!" Gertrude cried. A tree lay across the road. Calvin stopped the truck and just stared at the tree. After several seconds of stunned silence, Gertrude said, "Don't suppose you have a chainsaw?"

"No, do you?" Calvin said, his voice thick with sarcasm.

"I have four of them, three Husqvarnas and a Jonsered, but none of them are with me at the moment." She looked around the cab. "There are four of us. I think we can probably move it."

"I have a better idea," Calvin said. She looked at him. He was looking out his side window.

"Calvin, no!" Gertrude said, reading his mind. "What if we get stuck?"

"We're stuck now, Gertrude, and if they are behind us, we're running out of time." Without any further discussion, Calvin gave the truck some gas and pulled the wheel to the left. He drove straight into the woods. Gertrude could see his plan laid out in front of them, but she didn't know if they'd fit. The roots of the fallen tree jutted out from the road into the forest, looking like a large angry monster with a hundred arms. Several feet to the left of that stood another tree, this one massive. Gertrude knew Calvin was going to try to drive between the two, which meant driving *through* a healthy crop of brambles.

"Once you get in the tickletuppy, don't slow down," Gertrude said.

"I won't." And he accelerated.

Carlotta started praying in the backseat.

Gertrude sucked her gut in as if that would give them the extra inch they might need. Calvin nosed the front end of his truck into the gap, and Gertrude let out her breath. This was going to work. A loud scrape sounded to Gertrude's right, but Calvin didn't slow down. Calvin cussed, and Gertrude decided to let it go this time, under the circumstances. After a painful few seconds, the scraping ended, and they were free. They had successfully run the gauntlet. Calvin accelerated, and they banged over another rotten log that lay in their path—then they were back on the road. The two ladies in back erupted into cheers. Calvin gave Gertrude a giant smile. "Keep your eyes on the road. You might not get to rest on your laurels."

They continued on the road until Gertrude began to worry it was going to cease to be a road—but then it spilled out onto another dirt road, this one obviously more frequently travelled. Calvin turned left.

They met a few cars on this road, and each time, the foursome held their breath until they passed, but none of the vehicles were black SUVs or in any other way suspicious. At the next stop sign, Calvin said, "I know where we are. We're in Plainfield. I can get us to Moscow from here."

"Good," Gertrude said. "I'm hoping they don't know that's where we're going."

"I don't see how they could know. Dave had you smash your phone because they could track it, right? Not because they could hear your conversation?"

Gertrude thought for a second. Then, "I'm sure that's why. He wouldn't have said the address over the phone if he thought they were listening."

"I still can't believe he's going to meet us at all," Calvin said.

"Of course he is. He's Dave." Without warning, Gertrude reclined her seat with a thump. It smashed into Andrea's lap.

"Hey!" Andrea cried.

"Just going to take a quick nap," Gertrude said, rolling over onto her right side. "Wake me up when we get to Russia."

19

"What *is* this place?" Gertrude sat up, rubbing her eyes. She couldn't quite process what she was looking at. It looked like a scene out of one of those end-of-the-world television shows she avoided because they were too scary. They were on another dirt road, driving alongside a giant property with a dilapidated fence all around it. Every ten feet or so, the fence featured an ominous "KEEP OUT" sign, promising imminent danger.

"Whatever it is, it's spooky," Andrea said.

"It was a federal radar site," Calvin said. "The Air Force used to monitor for Russian aircraft here—"

"That's kind of funny," Andrea said.

"What's funny?" Gertrude said, annoyed that Andrea had interrupted Calvin.

"That they chose the town of Moscow to monitor the Russians."

"Anyway," Calvin continued, "they could scan from Greenland to Cuba. If a Russian plane was headed our way, this place would know it."

"And now what is it?" Gertrude asked.

"Don't know. Now I think it's nothing. Apparently, it's where Dave hangs out."

"It's huge," Gertrude said, trying to see through the fence as Calvin sped by.

"Over a thousand acres, if I remember correctly."

Finally, they came to a gate in the fence, and it was open. Gingerly, Calvin pulled in. He drove toward the closest building. As he approached, they saw Dave step into sight and wave them over toward the building. Calvin obeyed his hand signals, and ended up parked tight up against the building. The four travelers spilled out of the truck excitedly. As Gertrude limped around the front of the truck, Dave eyed them all warily.

"So not only did you risk all our lives contacting me against my wishes, but you also brought a whole carload of people to meet me. What part of 'I don't want to be found' do you have so much trouble with?"

"Sorry, Dave." Gertrude didn't sound even remotely sorry. "This was a matter of life and death—"

"Were you followed?"

"At first, yeah, but Calvin lost them."

Dave turned toward Calvin.

"Why here, Dave?" Calvin asked.

Dave held out his hands. "Middle of nowhere. Big open space. No one going to sneak up on us. And if they try, I've got friends watching." He pointed upward.

All four of them looked up. None of them saw anything. *Did he mean angels?*

"I don't see anyone," Calvin said.

"That's kind of the point. Now, let's make this quick. Who is in danger?"

Gertrude took a shaky step toward him. She hadn't taken the time to retrieve her walker from the bed of the truck and she was now regretting it. "A woman named Tallia Bachman, though she went by the name of Tally—"

"She *went*?" Dave interrupted. "As in she's dead?"

"I don't think she's dead. But she disappeared in 1995. She had a boyfriend named ..." Gertrude paused. She couldn't remember the guy's name.

"Tyson Ross," Calvin supplied.

"Yes, Tyson, so she might be Tally Ross by now. Anyway, her father lives in Clearwater. He owns a store marina thing. He's going to sell it. But what if Tallia wants it?"

Gertrude stopped talking, and Dave stood silent. Then, "That's it? Where's the life or death part?"

Gertrude shifted her weight nervously. "Well, people think she's dead, and she's not."

"People think she's dead?"

No one said anything. Gertrude feared she was losing control of the situation. "I have information that suggests she is *not* dead, and I just want to tell her that her father's about to sell the store."

"What information?" Dave said.

"I can't say."

"We're done here. Don't contact me again. If you pull that *Uncle Henry's* stunt, I will ignore it and let them do what they want to do with you."

Calvin groaned. "Look. I'm sorry, Dave. I didn't really understand how complicated your situation is, or I would have tried to stop her from reaching out. I *will* stop her from reaching out. But this time, we could use your help. We've got a weird situation on our hands. Someone is pretending to haunt a lake, pretending to be Tallia Bachman haunting a lake. This person is terrorizing our friend Carlotta here." He paused to point to Carlotta, who smiled sheepishly. "Gertrude thinks Tallia is alive. If she is, we could blow the whole scam out of the water, so to speak. And if she's really dead, and you could find that out, then that would give her father some closure."

Dave stayed silent for so long that Gertrude thought it was a lost cause. Then he cemented this idea when he said, "So you contacted me, someone who doesn't want to be found, so that I could help you find someone else who, if she isn't dead, doesn't want to be found."

"We don't know that she doesn't want to be found!" Gertrude cried, beyond frustrated. "She was just a child when she was taken. We don't know what happened to her!"

"She was taken?" Dave said quickly.

"Yes!" Gertrude said, though she had no idea if this was true.

Dave took a deep breath. "Tallia Bachman from Clearwater?"

Gertrude nodded eagerly.

"I'll see what I can find. But if I find she wants to stay gone, I'm going to respect that."

"Of course," Gertrude said.

"Yeah," Dave said, his voice full of doubt. "Give me another number where I can reach you, and then get out of here." Calvin and Carlotta hurried to the truck to find paper, which took them a very long time.

As they searched, Andrea asked, "Who *are* you?"

"I'm nobody."

"Are you like Jack Reacher?"

"No. Definitely not."

"Who's Jack Reacher?" Gertrude asked, but they both ignored her.

"Are you Jason Bourne?"

"No."

Andrea gasped. "Are you The Gray Man?"

"Gray Man?" Gertrude repeated quietly.

Dave chuckled. "No ... well, sort of. But I'm no assassin."

"The people after you—are they good guys or bad guys?"

"Depends on your perspective," Dave said. "But I assure you, I'm a good guy."

"I'm supposed to be the one asking questions, Andrea." Gertrude looked at Dave. "So, Dave, who are you?"

"Like I've said a dozen times—"

"Yeah, yeah, you are no one—well obviously, you're someone. You have lots of guns, you're good at being a hero, and you know how to find people."

Dave paused. "How *did* you know I could do that, by the way?"

Gertrude shrugged. "I just knew. You are a spook. Spooks have contacts. They can do things."

A small smile flickered across Dave's face. He took a deep breath. "I'm not a spook. But I did work for the government. Then I decided I didn't want to anymore. This upset some people. I know some things, and some people are worried I will share them." He stared off into the distance. "Which of course, I wouldn't. But still. They like to try to keep an eye on me."

"Why'd you quit?" Gertrude asked.

Dave's face lit up. "I found Jesus."

Andrea cackled. "Jesus? What does he have to do with anything?"

"My boss asked me to do something. Jesus asked me not to. That was the end of my career."

Calvin finally returned with a piece of paper with Carlotta's number on it and handed it over to Dave.

Dave took it and without looking at it, put it in his pocket. "If I find anything, I'll be in touch. If you don't hear from me, assume I didn't find anything."

"Or assume you did and you're not going to tell us," Gertrude said.

"Assume whatever you want. Just don't call me again. Now scram."

20

When the tired foursome got back to Carlotta's home, they found the red light on her answering machine blinking. She pressed the play button. The message was so short, she was the only one who heard it the first time through. She called everyone to gather around and pressed play again. "She's alive. She's at 10 Casper Drive in Christmas, Florida. Good luck." Click.

"Christmas?!" Gertrude said. "What kind of a town is that?"

"Could be worse. There's a town in Michigan called Hell." Calvin looked at Gertrude. "All right. I can't believe it, but apparently you were right. So now what?"

"Now we go to Florida."

Calvin guffawed. "I am not driving you to Florida."

Gertrude looked at the two women. Bewildered, they both shook their heads. "Fine then. I'll just take a bus."

Calvin gave her a long look. "You're really going to go?"

"I don't see what choice I have. He didn't leave her phone number."

Calvin nodded. "Well, then, let's fly."

"Fly? You mean like on a airplane?"

"No, a magic carpet. Yes, a plane."

"I've never been on an airplane before."

"Oh, don't worry, Gertrude," Carlotta cooed. "It's a piece of cake. You'll love it."

"Let me make some calls," Calvin said.

The women went into the living room and sat. Gertrude was exhausted. She wondered if there was such a thing as too much excitement, and then decided that no, there probably wasn't. She looked at Andrea. "If I'm going to Florida, can you watch my cats?"

"Of course."

As an afterthought, she added, "Can you watch Carlotta too?"

"Of course."

"Seriously. I think you should spend the night with her, in case Bon Jovi comes back."

"I will do that."

"I appreciate that, Andrea," Carlotta said. She was staring out the window, looking pensive. Gertrude, how did you know she was alive?"

"They never found the body."

"Still," she said, staring out at the lake. "And if she's alive, then who is haunting our lake?"

"Nobody is haunting your lake." Gertrude's eyes followed Carlotta's gaze. It was a Saturday, and the lake was chock-full of chipper children. "Someone is pretending to. But I don't know why. Yet." She looked at Carlotta all of a sudden. "How much did you say Vacationland offered you for this place?"

Carlotta flushed. "I'm embarrassed to say. You'll think I'm nuts for not selling."

"I won't think you're nuts. I never get too shook up over money. And what did you tell them exactly?"

"I told them that it didn't matter how much they of-fered—I wouldn't sell. Why?"

"I'm just wondering if maybe they're behind this. You said Eli Bachman didn't want to sell at first either, right? So then his daughter's ghost starts screaming in the middle of the night.

And then he's willing to sell? And then someone's singing outside your window? Do you see the pattern?"

"I don't think a company like Vacationland would behave that way," Carlotta said skeptically.

"Oh, don't say that!" Andrea said. "Gertrude's been after them for a while now. She can smell evil intent from a million miles away."

Calvin sauntered into the room. "We'd better get going. We've got a flight to catch."

"Seriously?" Gertrude said. She couldn't believe this was really happening. Was she really going to get on an airplane? She'd never even been out of the state of Maine. "Where are we going?"

Calvin scowled. "Florida, aren't we?"

"No, I mean, where are we going to get on the airplane?"

"Oh, Bangor. Direct flight from Bangor to Orlando. Cost me an arm and a leg, but I figure it will be worth it if we can reunite a father and daughter. I booked the return flight for tomorrow though. I don't want to leave Carlotta alone for long, so let's go and get back as quickly as possible."

"Do they really give you free peanuts?" Gertrude asked. She was starving.

"They're not really free if you pay a thousand dollars for your seat, but yes, I believe they still hand out the world's most expensive peanuts."

"Alrighty," Gertrude said, getting up. "Let's get going then. Christmas is calling."

Carlotta jumped up. "I'll pack you a snack bag to go. It'll be hours before you get those peanuts."

21

"Why are there so many airplanes?" Gertrude wondered aloud.

Calvin pulled into the parking lot of the Bangor airport, and Gertrude looked around with wide eyes.

Calvin hesitated before answering, as if he didn't know what to say. "Well, this is a pretty big airport. So lots of planes going to lots of places, I guess."

Still seemed like far too many to Gertrude. Where could they all be going? Did that many people live in Bangor? And were they all trying to get *out* of Bangor? All at once?

Calvin parked the truck, and they began the long walk to the terminal. At least they didn't have any baggage, just the snack bag, the contents of which Gertrude had already put quite a dent in.

Calvin printed out their boarding passes at a kiosk, and Gertrude was content to stand back and let him run this particular leg of the investigation. She wasn't about to admit it, but she was feeling a bit overwhelmed.

All of a sudden, Calvin looked at her in a panic. "You do have a photo ID, don't you?"

"Of course I do!"

His face fell in relief. "Oh good. I thought maybe, since you didn't have a driver's license, you might not have an ID." He looked anxious again. "And you have this photo ID with you?"

"Yes, Calvin! I'm not a cave man!"

She followed Calvin down a long hallway toward the gates. "We're going to have to go through security," he said quietly.

"Please try to act like a normal person. If you do anything suspicious, it's going to drag the process out."

"What do you mean? I always act normal!"

He looked at her. "You aren't even close to normal. And that's a good thing. But for right now, just try to pretend. And also—try to be polite."

She still didn't know what he meant exactly, but decided she would try. They waited in line for what seemed like eons, and she was just about to announce she no longer wanted to fly to The Sunshine State when they were finally beckoned to a podium by a sour-faced woman in uniform. She read Gertrude's boarding pass, looked at her ID, looked at Gertrude, looked at her ID again, and then stared at Gertrude. Gertrude wanted to say, "Is this a staring contest?" but she remembered Calvin's warning and decided to try to be polite.

Eventually, the woman in uniform handed Gertrude her paperwork and waved her toward the carry-on X-ray belt.

"You've got to take off your shoes," Calvin said, bending over to take his off.

"What?" Gertrude cried. "Why?"

"It's OK, ma'am," a man behind the belt said. He smiled at her. "If you have a disability, you can leave your shoes on."

She smiled at Calvin triumphantly.

He looked annoyed. "You didn't scold him for calling you ma'am," he mumbled.

"You told me to be polite," she mumbled back. She put her snack bag on the belt, and watched it travel toward the machine; then at the last second, she reached forward with both hands and stopped it.

The nice leave-your-shoes-on-ma'am man behind the belt raised an eyebrow.

"This is my food," she explained. "Are you going to zap it with radiation and make it poisonous?"

He laughed. "No, ma'am. Your food will be just fine."

"All right then," she said, letting go of the bag. She wasn't convinced though, and vowed not to eat the food.

"We'll need your walker as well, ma'am."

Gertrude was so surprised by this that she just stood there looking at the man.

"You can just stand right there until we scan it. Then we'll bring it right back to you."

"All right." Gertrude gently put her beloved walker on the belt. It made no sense, but this made her incredibly nervous, so she held her breath until the walker was safe in front of her, and she was safe behind it.

She was beckoned through the scanner, and she stepped into the arch. This made her feel a little like a secret agent and she giggled. The TSA agent looked at her suspiciously and then waved her through. *I'm free!*

There were no empty seats at the gate, which annoyed Gertrude, but they didn't have to wait there for long before they began boarding. Gertrude's stomach was doing somersaults. She was both excited and terrified. She was also too proud to admit to Calvin that she was nervous. So she tried to look confident as she followed him down the jetway.

22

"Calvin"—Gertrude leaned closer to whisper into his ear—"why are there so many people on the airplane?"

He shrugged. "They try to fill every seat. Empty seats don't make them any money."

Gertrude stood up and looked around the plane. Sure enough, she couldn't see any empty seats. She couldn't believe this many people wanted to go from Bangor to Orlando, and wondered what each of them was going for. What was so exciting about Orlando?

"Calvin?"

"Yes?" He looked annoyed.

"When do we get the peanuts?"

"I don't even know if we're going to get peanuts. Do you want me to get the snack bag?" He had put it in the overhead bin.

"No. They nuked our Cheetos."

Calvin didn't comment on this. Instead, he said, "Just try to relax. Sleep the way you do every time you get into a land-based vehicle. Then you'll wake up in Florida."

"I can't relax, Calvin. I'm on an airplane. This is exciting." She closed the window. Then opened it. Then closed it again. Then opened it.

"Stop."

"Fine." She took a magazine out of the seat pocket in front of her and began reading instructions for what to do in a crash. "Calvin?" She looked up at him. "Why is this magazine trying to scare me?"

Calvin took it away from her and shoved it back in the seat pocket. "Will you *please* just go to sleep?"

The pilot's voice, booming from the overhead and scaring her more than a little, announced his intention to takeoff. Gertrude braced herself. The engines roared, and the plane began to move. Gertrude grabbed her armrest with her right hand and Calvin's hand with her left and squeezed for dear life. She looked out the window. "We are going *really* fast!"

Then she felt it. Liftoff. "Weeeee!" she cried, loudly enough for most of the plane to hear. She eased her grip on both the seat and Calvin and looked out the window. She could see the airport below her, and it looked much smaller now. Then she could see all of Bangor, spread out below her. "The highway looks like a long noodle!" she said with delight. And then they were in the clouds. All she could see was white. How disappointing. She looked at Calvin. "Wake me up when there's something else to see." She leaned back and closed her eyes.

"Do you want me to wake you up for the peanuts?"

She opened one eye and looked at him. "Does a bear poop in the woods?"

Calvin shook his head and closed his own eyes.

"You can't go to sleep! We'll miss the peanuts!"

"I won't go to sleep. Just resting my eyes."

Unconvinced, Gertrude closed hers too, vowing she would stay awake. Twenty seconds later, she was sound asleep. Twenty minutes after that, Calvin gently shook her knee.

"Peanuts?" Her eyes popped open, and she sat up straight.

"Yes," Calvin said. "And would you like a drink?"

A flight attendant stood in front of Calvin, staring at Gertrude expectantly. She was smiling, but Gertrude could tell she was faking it. She could tell she hated her job, and wondered how anyone could hate anything as exciting as flying around all the time.

"Do you have Crystal Light?"

"No, sorry." She rattled off an impressive list of soft drinks.

"You have all those in that little cart there?"

"Yes, ma'am."

"I'll take a Fresca please. I like Fresca. It takes like fizzy grapefruit."

"I think that's the idea," Calvin muttered as the flight attendant dug through her drawer of cans.

Gertrude marveled that she could even open a can with nails that long, and then took the outstretched cup of soda. "That's it? I can't have the whole can?"

The woman's fake smile got even wider, and she handed her the can. "Peanuts?"

"Oh yes! Please! And could you turn the heat up?"

The woman handed her a tiny foil pack. "Sure."

Gertrude took the package. Then felt it with both hands. She looked at Calvin, appalled. "There's only like four peanuts in here!"

"I never said they gave you a *lot* of peanuts. Here, you can have mine too."

"Thanks. Now I have eight peanuts."

Calvin reached over and lowered her tray for her.

She put her drink—both the cup and the can—on it. "Thank you, Calvin." Then she had a better idea. She drained the cup in one long gulp, and then put the empty cup on Calvin's tray. Then she picked up her can and folded the tray shut. Then she opened it. And shut it. And opened it. She smiled at Calvin. "I need to get a few of these!"

"Aren't you going to eat the peanuts?"

She looked down at them in her lap. "I don't think so. They're pretty neat little packages. I think I'd rather just keep them. Maybe start a new collection."

A familiar cry sounded from somewhere behind her. Her head whipped around, but she couldn't see anything except for the seatback. She didn't dare unbuckle. The seatbelt light was still on. "Did you hear that?" she whispered.

"Hear what?"

"I could've sworn I just heard a cat."

He shrugged. "I didn't hear it, but it doesn't surprise me. Lots of people fly with their pets."

Gertrude's mouth fell open. "We could've brought my cats?!"

23

A few hours later, the plane descended out of the clouds. Gertrude gasped.

"What is it?" Calvin leaned over to look out the window.

"There are so many lights! Orlando is a big city! How many people live here, Calvin?"

"I don't know, Gert. Lots, I suppose."

The city's details grew bigger and bigger until she couldn't see anything but the airport. Then there was a jarring motion and a screeching sound and only then did she think to brace herself. She looked at Calvin. "Is that it?"

"That's it. We're on the ground. Not so bad, right?"

Though they were still taxiing, Gertrude unbuckled and stood abruptly. She turned around. "Who here has the cat?"

"Ma'am, you need to sit down!" a voice from the front hollered.

The woman seated behind Gertrude looked up at her with wide, frightened eyes.

"It's you, isn't it?" Gertrude said.

The woman nodded and said a shaky, "Why?"

"Ma'am! Sit down!"

Gertrude ignored the flight attendant. "I'd just like to meet him is all. Will you let me meet him before we get off the plane?"

The woman's face broke into a big smile. "Sure."

Gertrude turned and plunked back down into her seat and put her seatbelt back on.

Twenty minutes later, the seatbelt light turned off. Gertrude stood and turned again and was pleased to see the woman was sliding a pet carrier out from under her seat.

"The cat was *under* me the whole time?" Gertrude couldn't believe it.

The woman slid a trembling kitty out of the bag. "This is Buffy."

"Buffy!" Gertrude chortled. "Is she a vampire slayer?"

The women blinked, confused.

"Never mind," Gertrude said, reaching down to scratch under the cat's chin. "Is this her first flight?"

"It is."

"Mine too. It's nice to meet you, Buffy. Congrats on earning your wings." She turned and sat back down to wait for Calvin to retrieve her walker, which he did without her saying a word.

Once she had her security blanket, she followed Calvin off the plane. The flight attendant glared at Gertrude as she walked by. "Thanks for the peanuts!" she said and winked at her.

Up the jetway they went, and through the airport. Gertrude gazed around in wonder. "This is like a mall!"

"Only even more expensive," Calvin grumbled.

Gertrude had to hustle to keep up with him. "What's your hurry?"

Calvin slowed.

"Where are we going anyway? Gonna catch a cab?" The idea excited Gertrude.

"Cabs are filthy. And expensive. Let's rent a car. Then we'll try to find her place. Then we'll decide how to proceed."

She followed him to the rental car booth and tried to be patient as he argued with the poor rental car clerk. They didn't have any economy cars, and Calvin thought that because of this, he should be able to get a full-size car at the economy price. In the end, he made no progress, and signed on the dotted line for a Toyota Camry.

A man in a green polo drove the car around for them. They stepped outside.

"Golly, it is hot in Florida!" Gertrude exclaimed.

Calvin did not respond. The man in green attempted to introduce him to the car's features, but Calvin wouldn't allow it.

"I know how to drive, young man."

The Floridian acted as if he got that all the time, and left Calvin alone with the running car. Gertrude stowed her walker and then climbed into the car. She wiggled her nose. "Smells funny in here."

"We won't be in it for very long. Let me know if you see a service station. We need a map."

Gertrude had just decided there must not be any gas stations in Florida when she saw one. "Tally ho!" she cried, pointing.

"I see it, I see it." Calvin pulled in.

He was back in five minutes with fury in his eyes. "They charged me five dollars for a map! Five dollars! Can you believe it? Maps used to be free!" He unfolded it with a flourish and then began to study it.

"Find anything?" Gertrude asked five seconds later.

"Give me a second. Give me a second." He continued to scan. Gertrude couldn't stand the waiting and started clicking her tongue.

"Stop."

She stopped. "Do you need me to look?"

"Nope. I found it." He pointed to Christmas. "Can you read a map?"

"Of course I can read a map. First of all, I have an extensive collection. Second, I used them all the time for lawnsaleing before I got my jitterbug." Her face fell. "Guess I'll need to start using them again."

"We'll get you a new phone, Gertrude. All right, you hold this. Be my navigator. Take us to Christmas, Gert."

24

Calvin pulled the Camry to the curb in front of 10 Casper Drive, which was a small, neat ranch. Though it was getting late into the evening, several lights were still on.

"Now what?" Calvin said.

"Now we go knock on Tally's door," Gertrude said as she opened the car door. She was already halfway up the walk before Calvin caught up to her.

"Do you have a plan?"

"I always have a plan." She rang the doorbell. Ten seconds later, she rang it again.

"Easy," Calvin said.

The door opened a crack. A woman peeked out at them from behind a security chain. "Can I help you?"

"Are you Tallia?"

"Yes."

From inside the house, a man hollered, "Who is it, Tally?"

"Is that Tyson?" Gertrude asked.

The woman flinched. "Who *are* you?" What little they could see of her face had drained of color.

"I'm sorry, Tally," Gertrude said. "We don't mean to scare you. We are here to help. We're friends of your father."

"My father?" She laughed humorlessly. "Is this some kind of joke?"

"Uh ... no." Gertrude couldn't imagine what she'd said to suggest she was trying to be funny. She never tried to be funny, certainly not now.

"My father's dead." She slammed the door.

Gertrude looked at Calvin. "What?" She pounded on the door. "Open up, Tally!" she yelled. "Eli's not dead! He's just old!"

The door opened again, and this time the face wore a beard. "What do you want?"

Gertrude cleared her throat and announced, "My name is Gertrude. I'm a gumshoe. Eli Bachman thinks his daughter is dead. Tally thinks her father is dead. I have come all the way from Maine, on an actual airplane, to tell everyone that no one is dead." She paused. Then added, less definitively, "Well, some people are dead, somewhere, but not these two ... people ... in question."

At first the man didn't do or say anything. Then he slid the chain out of its notch and opened the door. "Come on in," he said. Then, "Tally, come here, honey. I think you're going to want to hear this." He held his hand out to Calvin. "I'm Mike Tree."

Gertrude snorted.

Calvin gave her a scolding frown.

"His name is Tree, and he lives in Christmas."

Calvin looked at Mike apologetically.

"It's OK, I get that a lot."

Feeling a bit miffed that *she* didn't get a handshake, Gertrude followed Mike into a tidy living room. A teenager wearing giant headphones looked up at them and then looked back down at her tablet.

"Have a seat," Mike Tree said, pointing toward a couch. Gertrude and Calvin sat. Tally came into the room timidly and sat down on an ottoman, as if her teen's daughter's feet weren't resting there. The teen pitched a fit about having to move her feet one foot to the left. Tally didn't seem to notice her teen's protest. This made Gertrude like Tally. *That's right, Tally. Be in charge.*

"So!" Gertrude rubbed her hands together. "You thought your father was dead?"

Tally nodded, tears welling up in her eyes. "I ran away when I was seventeen. I was pregnant." Gertrude looked at the teenager. The math didn't seem to work. Tally read Gertrude's expression. "No, no. This is Ashley. She's Mike's and my daughter. My oldest, Elisha, doesn't live with us. She's all grown up." Her voice cracked on these last few words. "Anyway, not long after I left home, my father killed himself." She paused and looked at Gertrude. "At least, that's what I've always thought."

"Did you think that because Tyson told you that?"

She nodded and rubbed her temple. "Oh wow, I've been such a fool."

Mike crossed the room and rubbed her back. "Elisha's biological father was abusive—both physically and psychologically. I met Tally when Elisha was three. Tally and I got married a year later, and I adopted Elisha. Tally here has worked hard and has done a lot of healing, but we don't talk about Tyson much anymore."

Tally looked up at him, her cheeks wet. "But my father might have been alive this *whole time*?"

"Not might be. He *is* alive," Gertrude said.

"And he thinks I'm dead?" The steadiness of Tally's gaze was unnerving.

"Yes. The morning after you left, he found your canoe upside down in the lake. Your flip-flops were floating nearby. And Tyson told your father that he didn't know where you were.

When you didn't turn up, your father assumed you drowned. Everyone did."

Tally stood up abruptly. "I have to get to him. I have to tell him I'm sorry. I have to ..." She was overcome by sobs, and Mike wrapped his arms around her. As she buried her face in his chest, Ashley removed her headphones.

"What's going on?"

"You need to go to Maine," Mike said. "Do you want us to go with you?"

"You have to work tomorrow," she said through sniffs.

"I can take a day off."

She looked around. "I think we should all go. I think we should get Elisha too."

Mike nodded. "I'll call the office. Then I'll get us some plane tickets."

Mike left the room.

"We're going to Maine?" Ashley said. "But I'm supposed to sing in church tomorrow!"

"Well, you're going to have to postpone your performance."

Ashley looked around the room. "Mom, what's going on?"

Tally put her hand on her daughter's knee. "Oh, sweetie, it's a long story ... but here's the short version. When I was your age, I got mixed up with a not very nice boy, and I got pregnant with your sister. I knew my dad would freak out, and I was so scared that I let my boyfriend talk me into running away with him. He promised me he would take care of me. He lied. He was awful, and he treated me horribly, and it was very hard for me to get away from him, but I did ... Don't be scared, Ash. The man has been dead for years. The point is, the only reason all of this is coming up now, is that one of the awful things this man did was tell me that my father killed himself. But it wasn't true, I guess. But ... I believed him."

"Oh, Mom ... I'm so sorry."

"It's OK. Go pack a bag. You're going to meet your grampa."

Ashley stood up, gave her mom a long hug, and then disappeared.

Mike came back into the room. "No more flights out until six a.m."

"Did you get tickets for that flight?" Tally asked.

"I did. Four of them."

"Would you mind telling me which flight?" Calvin asked. "I'll make sure we're on the same one."

"Sure thing," Mike said.

As he and Calvin talked flight numbers, Tally looked at Gertrude. "Do you have a place to stay the night?"

"Not yet."

"We have a guest room, and you are welcome to it."

"What about Calvin?"

Tally looked confused. "He's welcome to stay too."

"Do you have two guest rooms?"

Tally hesitated. Then, "Oh! I'm sorry! I just assumed you two were married."

"No. We're not married. We're just partners."

Tally frowned.

"*Investigative* partners," Gertrude clarified.

"Oh! I see. Well, I can't tell you how grateful I am for you coming all this way. Can I ask ... why didn't you just call?"

"I thought maybe you didn't want to be found. Like you were hiding out. I was going to try to convince you to come out into the open. Your dad is about to sell the store, and I wanted you to know about it, in case you didn't want him to, in case you wanted to try to talk him out of it."

"I see. Wow. Information overload!" She tittered. "You are welcome to the guest room. We only have one room, but I'll offer Calvin the couch. And then, tomorrow morning, we'll head to Maine. I can't even believe it."

25

Twelve hours later, Calvin pulled his pickup truck into Happy Trout's small parking lot. Mike Tree pulled in right behind him in a rental car. The six of them spilled out and headed into the store. Gertrude made sure she was the first one through the door. She wanted as much of the glory as possible. "Hi, Isabel!" she called out as soon as she was inside. "Where's Eli?"

"Why?" Isabel said protectively.

"Because we need to see him. It's a matter of life and death." Isabel didn't move. "Right now." Isabel still didn't move. "Tell him I'm suing him because his dynamites gave me an ulcer."

Isabel turned and left through a door in the kitchen.

Eli appeared only seconds later, looking like a man on a warpath. "What is going on?"

"Eli," Gertrude said, "your daughter isn't dead. She's right here." She stepped aside.

Eli looked past Gertrude to the family of four standing in his store. At first he didn't say anything. Then he said, so softly it was difficult to hear him, "Tallia? ... My little *kibsa*?"

"Dad!" Tally burst into tears and ran to the counter.

Eli came around it just as fast as he could and met her en route, throwing his big arms around his daughter. "Tally," he cried, stroking her hair. "I thought you were gone." They held each other for several minutes as the onlookers stood awkwardly wiping at their own eyes.

Finally, Tally pulled away and looked up at her father's weathered face. "I'm so sorry, Dad. I'll explain later. So much has happened ... but I didn't mean to stay away for so long. I thought you were dead." She took a deep breath. "I'll get to all that, but first, Dad, please let me introduce you to your family. This is my husband, Mike. And these are your granddaughters, Ashley and Elisha—she's named after you."

Eli spread his arms wide and pulled all of them into a clumsy but beautiful embrace.

Gertrude let them hug it out for as long as she could stand it, and then cleared her throat. "Excuse me, everyone, but there's something we didn't tell you yet."

Tally wiped at her eyes. "What more could there possibly be?"

"Well ... someone is pretending to be your ghost, and since you're not dead, it's obviously not you."

"What?" Tally's eyes were as big as saucers.

"You heard me right. Someone's been screaming at night and singing Bon Jovi and walking around in a glow-in-the-dark dress. I think someone is trying to scare your father, and another friend of ours, and they are pretending that your ghost is haunting this lake. So here's what I need from you. Don't tell anyone you're back. Just give me a little while to catch the fake ghost. If everyone finds out you're here, I'm afraid the fake ghost will hit the road, and I'll never catch her."

Tally nodded, looking bewildered. "Why would someone be trying to scare my father?"

"We don't really know. But I think whoever it is might be after the store."

Tally looked up at him. "Do you want to sell the store?"

"No, *kibsa*, I want to give it to you."

"See?" Gertrude said gravely. "It's talk like that that will scare the ghost off. So can you just stay hidden for a bit while I catch her red-handed?"

"OK, yeah, sure."

"Why don't we all go upstairs?" Eli said. "We'll catch up. And lay low." He nodded at Gertrude. "You do your thing." Then he looked over his shoulder at Isabel. "Could you bring us up some dynamites?"

"And some extra H20!" Gertrude added. "They're going to need it."

Eli began to lead everyone up a flight of stairs, but Tallia turned away from the crowd and came to Gertrude.

She took one of Gertrude's hands in both of hers, looked her in the eye, and said, "I don't know how I'll ever thank you. But how did you know? If everyone thought I was dead, what made you think I wasn't?"

Gertrude shrugged. *There was no body.* "I just knew."

"I'm sure glad you did. And how did you find me? I haven't used my maiden name in a very long time."

"Sorry," Gertrude said. "If I told you that, it would put you in danger."

Tally started, but then relaxed. "You are one-of-a-kind, aren't you, Gertrude?"

"I'm the only one I've ever met."

26

"Now what?" Carlotta asked, after serving Calvin and Gertrude giant deli-style sandwiches and iced sweet tea.

Gertrude took a big bite and then said through a full mouth, "Did you guys hear or see anything while we were gone?"

Andrea nodded enthusiastically. "The singer returned."

"What?" Gertrude screeched.

"Yeah, but as soon as I heard her, I flung open the window and stuck my head out."

Gertrude was impressed. "Wowsa, Andrea! Good for you! Did you see her?"

"I didn't get a good look. It was so dark, but she was definitely a she. And she was wearing a flimsy white dress."

"Same song?" Calvin asked.

"Yep!" Andrea said. "So how do we catch her?"

"I think it's time I go back out and sleep on the shore," Gertrude said. "And this time we hope there's no hurricane."

"Are you sure, Gertrude?"

"Yes, Calvin. I'll be fine. Unless it rains."

"Can I please go with you this time?"

Gertrude thought it over. She kind of did want him to go with her. But she wanted all the credit. But she could use the help. "Sure. You can come. As long as you don't get in my way. But first I'm going to finish my sandwich. And then I'm going to take a nap."

She finished her feast and then stretched out on the couch. "Someone wake me up before dusk."

Calvin woke Gertrude several hours later by shaking her shoulder.

"Ahh!" she grumbled, pushing his hand away. "I'm up, I'm up."

"Rise and shine. Time to go to work."

"Yeah, yeah." She sat up and rubbed her eyes. "Do you think Carlotta would make us some coffee, even though it's not morning?"

"Two steps ahead of you," Calvin said, holding up a thermos.

"Ah, excellent." Gertrude got up and saw that Calvin had already packed a bag of supplies. She looked at him. "Sleeping bags?"

"Yes."

"Pillows?"

"Check."

"Flashlights?"

"And extra batteries."

"Rope?"

"What do we need rope for?"

"To tie up the ghost, silly."

Calvin turned toward Carlotta. "Do you have any rope?"

"I'll see what I can do." She vanished and came back a minute later with two skeins of yarn.

"Yarn?" Gertrude cried.

"Just double up. It's tough stuff." She stuffed it into their bag.

"All right. I think that's it," Calvin said. "Let's go, Gertrude."

"Wait!" Carlotta cried. "There's one more thing." She scooted into the kitchen. Gertrude followed. She pulled something out of an AmeriCell bag. "This morning, Andrea and I went and got you a new smartphone, Gertrude. You'll have to call them to connect it to your number, but they said that would only take a few minutes. You'd better do that before you go, in case you need to call for a ride again."

Gertrude was touched. She hadn't realized how much Carlotta cared about her and her cellular needs. "Thanks, Carlotta! You're the cat's meow."

"Wow!" Calvin exclaimed. "That's high praise coming from Gert."

Carlotta beamed. "I figured as much. Now you two daredevils get out of here, before I think too much about what you're doing."

Calvin skipped the driveway they'd used the last time Gertrude had gone on a ghost-watching stakeout and took the next one, because he said it looked less traveled. The long drive led to an old camp in need of some TLC. Gertrude was disappointed to see it didn't have a deck.

"Don't worry," Calvin said, pointing to a large evergreen. "We can just set up camp under that tree. If it rains, we're going home anyway, right?"

"Yes, but I wanted to camp somewhere where she can't see us."

"She won't be able to see us. We'll hunker down, and it'll be dark. Come on, let's go get set up."

Gertrude let him do most of the work. He rolled out the tarps and the bedding and then handed her a snack bag she didn't know he'd brought.

"We'd better make sure we don't fall asleep before eating all this. Don't want to attract killer raccoons."

Calvin laughed. "*Killer* raccoons?"

"Oh yes, they're vicious." Gertrude plopped down and opened a granola bar. Then she poured herself a cup of coffee.

Calvin sat down and leaned against a tree. "Well, this isn't very comfortable."

"No, it's not. But we're going to catch her this time. I can feel it. Then we'll get to be heroes. Or, at least I will be."

"Gertrude, I need to tell you something."

He sounded so serious, it alarmed her, and she looked over at him quickly, but she couldn't see him as it was growing dark so fast. "What?"

"Carlotta told me that she thought maybe you were a little jealous."

"What?"

"Shh! First of all, let me finish. Second, don't give away our position. And so, I just wanted to tell you that ... I do think the world of Carlotta. She's a wonderful woman, and there was a time when I was sweet on her. But that was a long time ago. She was a part of who I used to be. But Gertrude, you're a part of who *I am now*."

Gertrude felt her eyes grow wide. She opened her mouth to say something, but she had no words.

"You have breathed life back into these old bones, Gertrude, and I am so grateful for that. So yes, once upon a time, I was sweet on Carlotta ... but now ... if I'm not too old to be sweet on someone, then I guess I am a little sweet on you."

Gertrude's mouth still hung open. She closed it. She opened it again. But nothing came out. So she just drank her coffee. As she did, she looked out toward the lake. "Oh Mylanta!" she cried.

"It's all right. I'm sorry, I didn't mean to make you uncomfortable."

"No, no, not that." She waved him off. "I just saw her."

"Already? It's barely dark out."

"She just went into that camper."

"How do you know it was her?"

"She was wearing the same dress. Come on, let's get closer." Without waiting for Calvin, she grabbed her walker and started creeping through the woods. Soon he was right behind her. She got as close to the camper as she dared, and then she ducked behind a boulder. She patted the ground beside her. Calvin sat on the ground and leaned against the rock.

"Now what?" he hissed.

"Now we wait for her to come out."

27

Ten minutes after midnight, when Calvin kept moaning because his back hurt, and Gertrude could not feel either of her legs, the camper door squeaked open.

Gertrude stopped breathing and squeezed Calvin's knee. He groaned, and she realized she might be squeezing too hard. She let go and pointed. He nodded. His expression said he was beyond caring though.

The woman in white stepped out into the darkness. The moonlight was weak, and Gertrude squinted to try to stay focused on her as she walked toward the water.

The woman slowly and gracefully strode all the way to the water, and then stepped into the water and stopped. *What on earth is she up to?* Then the pseudo-apparition touched her waist with her right hand, and instantly her whole dress lit up with an unearthly glow. Gertrude gasped. "That's a neat trick." Then, without another word, Gertrude leapt out of her hiding spot. Every joint in her body screamed in protest. *Where's that kick of adrenaline I was counting on?*

"Gertrude!" Calvin hissed, and Gertrude knew that tone. It meant: what are you doing?

Leaning heavily on her walker, she hurried toward the phony phantom, who, Gertrude thought, had to be the most unobservant criminal ever—she knew she wasn't being very quiet as she walker-galloped toward the water. As she neared the water, she realized the gentle lapping of the water on the shore had probably covered her noise. Just as she was mere feet away, just as she lifted her walker up over her head with both hands, the woman finally turned to look, and Gertrude brought the walker down with all her might, effectively clobbering the woman.

She threw her hands up, but not in time to stop the blow, and she cried out in surprise and pain as she staggered deeper into the water. But she didn't fall. And much to Gertrude's dismay, she took off running—through the water. Fueled by instinct alone, Gertrude took off after her, clumsily splashing through the water, screaming, "Freeeeeeze"!

The fraud did not freeze, and Gertrude was about to give up when the woman tripped and fell face first into the lake.

"Ahhhhhh!" Gertrude screamed as she leapt through the air and came down on top of her future prisoner with a mighty splash. Gertrude's mouth filled with water, and she came up coughing and clutching her chest. The woman sat up, pushed the hair out of her face, and asked, "Are you all right?"

Gertrude coughed, and said through a watery voice, "My, you are a sweet criminal."

"I'm not a criminal, I swear!"

"What are you then?"

"I'm an actress!"

Gertrude cackled. "Can't wait to see this on your resume. Stand up, and please don't run again. I'm exhausted, and the ruse is up." The woman stood, and Gertrude, much more slowly, joined her in verticality. "Calvin!" she screamed. "Bring the yarn!" Then she looked at the woman. "Follow me." Gertrude looked around for her walker, and didn't see it. She started to panic. Had it floated away?

"Follow you? Are you going to move?"

"Zip it, lassie. I'm looking for my walker."

The woman turned off her dress. "There. That should make it easier to see."

She's not wrong, Gertrude thought as her eyes adjusted.

"I see it!" she said, and splashed away from Gertrude, deeper into the water. For a second, Gertrude thought she was trying to escape, but then she turned and headed back toward Gertrude with walker in tow.

"Oh, thank God," Gertrude muttered.

"Gertrude?" Calvin said.

She turned to the sound of his voice and was instantly blinded by his flashlight beam.

"I have the yarn."

Gertrude looked at the woman as she handed her the walker. "What's your name, Casper?"

"Danica Rose."

"Sure, that sounds real. Do we have to tie you up, Danica Rose, or will you walk to the truck with us like a nice girl?"

"Your truck? I'm not getting in some strange truck in the middle of the night."

"Wow, that sounds like a really wise decision coming from a woman pretending to haunt a lake in the middle of the night."

The actress didn't say anything.

"Cat got your tongue? All right, Calvin, give me the yarn. Missy, put your hands behind your back."

"Fine, fine. Where do you want to take me?"

"Just to the other side of the lake. Come on, let's go."

The two women turned toward the flashlight and stepped out of the lake.

"Just follow the light, lassie, just follow the light."

28

Four of them sat in Carlotta's living room. Carlotta stood in the doorway, leaning on the wall, her arms folded across her chest, glaring at the woman in white, who was now also wrapped in a white blanket Carlotta had graciously provided.

"All right," Gertrude said. "Spill it. Tell us everything."

The woman looked around nervously. "There's not much to tell."

"You can start with the part where you sang outside my window like some kind of stalker."

Danica flushed. "I'm sorry. I was really uncomfortable with that part." She looked around at all the glaring faces. "Look, I'm just an actress. I needed the money—"

"What kind of an actress lives in Clearwater?"

"Don't interrupt her, Gertrude," Calvin said.

"I don't live here. I'm from Boston. I just came here for the gig, which pays very well, by the way." She stopped.

"And what was the gig exactly?" Gertrude prodded.

"I was supposed to walk along the shore at night wearing this dress. And then once I'd already gotten started, they added the part about singing outside your window." She looked at Carlotta. "I'm sorry if I scared you."

"Sure." Carlotta didn't sound convinced.

"Am I in trouble?"

"That depends. Who hired you?"

"I don't know."

Gertrude guffawed. "Classic. Well, who paid you?"

"I don't know. Money was sent online from an email that didn't even make sense. Just a bunch of numbers and letters. Everything was done by email."

"And that didn't strike you as suspicious?" Gertrude asked.

"Maybe, but it's not like I was hurting someone. I just did my job and got paid well for it."

"Good, you can buy good snacks while you're in the slammer."

"What?" the girl shrieked. "You said I wasn't in trouble!"

"I said no such thing," Gertrude said. "But I'll tell you what. You're going to call the Sheriff's Department right now, and you're going to turn yourself in. And you're going to stay here until they come to get you. And you're not going to tell them anything about me. I'm assuming you don't want to admit you got beaten up by a lady with a walker. So just pretend this surrender was all your idea. Should help your cause."

"Gertrude?" Calvin said, surprised.

"We'll hide in the bedroom. I just don't think Hale needs to know I was involved in this particular case." She looked at Carlotta. "I'm in a wee bit of trouble for operating without a license, or some foolishness, and I'll be getting a license soon, but I don't exactly have it yet." She looked at Danica Rose. "I've been too busy chasing *ghosts.*"

"So you're taking a page out of Dave's playbook?" Calvin said.

"No," Gertrude snapped. "I am smart enough to come up with my own ideas."

"You might want to hide in the basement," Carlotta said. "You'll be able to hear better from down there." She looked at Danica. "Go sit by that heating grate, so they can hear you bet-

ter, and if you say anything to give them away, I will make my
testimony much more damaging."

Danica didn't look appropriately scared.

So Carlotta continued. "I'll just add that you had a
weapon, and that you threatened to kill me and all my grandchildren."

Wowsa, Carlotta's not so sweet anymore.

"What?" Danica screeched.

"So you don't mention Gertrude or Calvin. Got it?"

Danica nodded, and moved to the chair closest to the air
vent.

Carlotta vanished and then returned within seconds with
a cordless phone, and a trembling actress made the call.

Gertrude and Calvin waited until the cops pulled into the
driveway, and then scampered downstairs. Gertrude flicked the
light on, and then Calvin turned it back off. "Let's not call any
attention to ourselves." He took her hand and led her through
the dark to the correct heating vent.

She was suddenly very uncomfortable with Calvin. Alone
in the dark. "Calvin? About what you said about being
sweet—"

"Shh! No time for that now."

Well, that was rude. Not going to bring that up again.

They heard footsteps, and then they heard two men introduce themselves: Deputy Hale and Deputy Dunlap. Carlotta
was right—they *could* hear everything. "You said on the phone
that you were hired to scare this woman?" Hale said. There was
a pause, and then he asked, "And who would want to do a thing
like that?"

"We think maybe Vacationland Development," Andrea said. "They've been buying up properties on either side of Carlotta's home, and they've been trying to buy this place for months."

"Hey," Dunlap said. "I remember you from Gunslinger City. Aren't you Gertrude's friend?"

Gertrude stiffened.

"I am Gertrude's friend," Andrea said, "and I am also Carlotta's friend. Aren't I allowed to have more than one friend?"

Nicely played, Andrea.

"And what are you doing here in the middle of the night?" Hale asked, sounding aggressively suspicious.

"I asked her to spend the night, because I was scared," Carlotta said quickly.

"OK," Hale said, "just don't want this unprofessional investigating to spread."

"Oh, I could never do what Gertrude does," Andrea trilled. "She's so brave and clever!"

Good job, Andrea. But don't lay it on too thick there.

"You say you communicated via email with the person who hired you?"

"Yes." The actress sounded terrified. This gave Gertrude some satisfaction.

"And you still have those emails?"

"Yes."

"Good. The truth is, the State Police are already investigating Vacationland. Several people all around the state have accused them of bullying people into selling things they don't want to sell. So there's a good chance they're behind this, and these emails might just be the evidence we need to get them."

"They also set me up with the camper," Danica said. "It's on the other side of the lake. When I got here, it was already there, so someone must have paid for all that."

"And no one thought it was weird that a camper appeared in someone's yard?" Hale asked.

"It wasn't in someone's yard. It was between camps—"

"Probably on land that Vacationland already bought," Andrea said, which was exactly what Gertrude was thinking.

"OK," Hale said, "let's get you down to the station."

There was a rustling noise that Gertrude assumed was Danica standing up.

"Why are you all wet?" Hale sounded startled.

"I fell in the lake."

"So you were walking along the lake, trying to scare people, and then you fell in, and then you just decided to turn yourself in?"

"I had a crisis of conscience," she said in a tone that didn't sound even remotely believable.

Not a very good actress up close, is she?

"OK, let's go," Hale said.

There were lots of footsteps, and then Hale said, from farther away, "If you need anything else from us, ma'am, just give us a call."

"Thank you," Carlotta said.

They waited another few minutes until the basement door opened, and Carlotta called, "It's safe!" She flipped the light on.

Ascending the steps, Gertrude felt a little sick that no one was going to know how smart she'd been in figuring all this out. Hale didn't even know about Tallia being alive. But then she decided that was a small price to pay to avoid being the cellmate of Danica Rose.

29

"Did you mean it when you said you were going to get licensed?" Andrea asked.

"I don't say things I don't mean."

"How long is it going to take? What's it going to cost? How hard is it?"

Gertrude looked at Andrea. "Do *you* want to get licensed?"

Andrea shrugged. "Maybe?"

This idea didn't bother Gertrude as much as she'd thought it would. Maybe it would be good to have a licensed assistant. Maybe they should all get licensed. Then Hale would never be able to mess with them. "First we need to get sixty hours of college credits in crime. Then we need to follow around a licensed investigator for twelve hundred hours. Then we pass a test. Easy peasy."

As Gertrude talked, Andrea's eyes grew wider and wider. "Gertrude, that sounds ... *impossible*."

"Nah," Gertrude said. "It won't be quick, but we'll be OK."

"Quick? It's going to take *years*! I could die of old age before I get licensed."

"Don't be a Debbie Downer. We'll be fine. Or ... we could move to South Dakota. They don't require licensing, and we probably wouldn't keep bumping into Hale there."

Andrea looked as though she was actually considering it. She looked at Calvin. "Would you move to South Dakota with us?"

"No!" Calvin barked. "Don't be ridiculous."

Gertrude leaned toward Andrea. "I can talk him into it."

"Is there even any crime in South Dakota?" Carlotta asked.

"If there is, Gertrude will manage to find it," Calvin said.

"Well, that's too bad," Carlotta said. "I was going to ask you if I could help you out, you know, join your team, but I can't move to South Dakota, because of the grandkids."

"No one is moving to South Dakota!" Calvin said with unnecessary volume.

"Never say never," Gertrude said. "But we're not done with this case yet."

"We're not?" Calvin said.

"No. You heard Hale. They don't really have any evidence against Vacationland, but I think I know where we can get some."

"Where?" Calvin was incredulous.

"Did you notice that our little actress never mentioned the screaming?"

Calvin nodded, looking thoughtful. "Now that you mention it."

"I don't think she's the one who did it. Come on, Calvin, we're going back into the paddleboat."

Calvin groaned. "Please, no."

"Don't worry, I've got a plan. I'm going to stack some pillows under my buttocks so I don't get stuck again."

Calvin laughed. "All right. Where are we going?"

"Back to the float. Come on. Bring the flashlights."

Andrea and Carlotta followed them outside. "Sure do wish I'd purchased a four-person paddleboat."

Gertrude climbed into the paddleboat like an old pro. Calvin was a bit more tentative, but he did manage to get aboard. "I don't think I've been this tired in my whole life."

"We can sleep when we're dead, Calvin."

Carlotta untied the boat and threw the rope to Calvin, who missed it entirely, but then pulled it in out of the water, dripping cold water into Gertrude's lap.

"Let's not talk about dying as we paddle out into a haunted lake in the middle of the night."

"The lake's not haunted, Calvin. And could you stop getting me all wet?"

The boat drifted away from shore, and they began to pedal.

"It's so quiet," Calvin whispered.

"Yes, creepy."

A loon sounded, and they both jumped.

"That's a much more beautiful sound when you're snug in your bed listening to it," Calvin said softly.

Gertrude scrunched up her face. "I don't like birds."

Calvin chuckled softly. "I can't tell if we're going in a straight line." They were both shining their flashlights straight ahead, but all they lit up was water.

"Where's the moon when you need it?" Gertrude said.

"Behind the clouds."

A bone-chilling scream split the silence wide open.

"Ahhhh!" Gertrude screamed and started paddling madly to get away from whatever it was that was promising to drown her.

"Stop!" Calvin put a firm hand on her knee. "We need to turn left."

"Why?"

"Because that's where the scream came from."

"Why do you want to turn toward the scream?" Gertrude's heart was racing so fast, she was afraid it was going to leap out of her chest.

"The lake's not haunted, remember? Now start paddling, slowly, so we turn left."

She started pedaling. He did not.

"I see it!" he said quietly, but triumphantly, shining his flashlight on the float. It was only about fifty feet away. Calvin started pedaling. The float crept closer.

"If that scream goes off again, I think I'm going to die. Feed my cats."

Calvin reached out and grabbed the float, and then pulled them around to the side where Gertrude had found the duct tape residue. "Well looky there," he said softly.

"Don't touch it!" she said quickly. She reached into her pocket. "I've got a Ziploc." She handed it to Calvin, and he opened it and wrapped it around his hand. Then he reached for the black square taped to the float. He pulled it off the float, and the sound of duct tape ripping off the hard plastic sounded supernaturally loud in the stillness. He shone his flashlight on the object in his hand.

"It's a sound effects machine. There are buttons for scream, sheep, and flatulence."

"Does it really say 'flatulence'?"

"No. I edited for civility. They must put it out here at night, and take it in every morning, or we would've found it last time. Or one of the thousands of kids who jump off this float would have." He looked around as if expecting someone in scuba gear to leap out of the water.

"Come on, let's pedal. Carlotta's going to have to make another phone call to Hale."

30

The following evening, it was all over the local news. A Vacationland Development agent by the name of Terance Dexter had been arrested and was facing charges of criminal threatening and terrorizing. Local woman Carlotta Grimes had found a sound effects machine taped to the float. There was no fingerprint evidence, but Terance had ordered the same machine online a month earlier. State Police were still investigating how high up the chain of command the conspiracy went. Vacationland Development had planned to turn that area of the Clearwater's shoreline into a high end resort.

"We got 'em," Gertrude said, stroking Storm's head. "Mama didn't get much credit this time, but we got the bad guys just the same." She made a mental note to make sure to tell her friend Anna the good news the next time she went to visit her in the hospital. Anna wasn't a big fan of Vacationland either. They'd practically stolen her apartment right out from under her.

A sharp knock on the door startled Gertrude. "Sorry, Storm. Gotta get that. Could be my next case." She gently set Storm on the floor and then got up and made her way to the door. She opened it to see two men in black suits and sunglasses. It was too dark out for sunglasses.

"Are you here to hire me?"

"Ma'am, we are with the FBI." They flashed badges so fast, they could have been toy stars handed out at Gunslinger City.

"And?"

"And we're looking for a fugitive we believe you know as Dave. May we come in?"

"No, you may not. And I don't know anyone named Dave."

"Ma'am, we know that's not true. You're not in any trouble. We just need to ask you a few questions. For your own protection."

"Can I have your badge numbers, please?"

"That's not necessary, ma'am."

"Please stop calling me ma'am. I am not old. And if I can't have your badge numbers, why don't you give me your names, which you haven't done yet, and then the name and phone number of your immediate supervisor?"

The men hesitated.

"A woman can't be too careful."

The one who hadn't yet spoken said, "Just tell us what you know about Dave's whereabouts, and we'll be out of your hair."

"For the last time, I don't know anyone named Dave. I'm shutting the door now and I'm calling the real police. Good night." She shut the door, locked it, and put a hand to her chest. Her heart was pounding. She peeked out a window and watched the men climb into a black SUV and drive away. She scrambled for some paper and wrote down the license plate number. They weren't even government plates. What terrible fakers.

She grabbed a jar of pickles out of the fridge and returned to her recliner. Storm returned to her lap, and Gertrude started a new episode of *Longmire*. She thought he was the handsomest man on television. She was wondering how hard it was to get a PI license in Wyoming when she nodded off, her open pickle jar in one hand.

Her ringing landline woke her nearly an hour later. She jerked, spilling pickle juice all over Storm. He jumped up and fled. "Sorry, shnookums." She got up and headed for the phone.

"Hello?"

"Hi, Gertrude. This is Carlotta."

"Oh, hi, Carlotta!" She wasn't expecting to hear from her so soon—or ever. "What can I do for you? Did you want to invite me to a Bon Jovi concert?" She laughed at her own joke.

"Dave just called me. He asked me to tell you, and this is his exact message: Nicely done, Gertrude, and don't worry, I've taken care of it. They won't be back."

"Wowsa, that sounds ominous."

"It sure does. Do you know what he's talking about?"

"Nah"—no use giving Carlotta more information than she needed—"but I'm not going to worry about it. Sounds like he has everything under control. Thanks for delivering the message."

Gertrude hung up and dialed Calvin.

"Hello?"

"I need to tell you about the men in black. Want to buy me supper?"

"Gertrude, it's half past seven. I've already eaten."

"So? I haven't."

He chuckled. "Sure, I'd love to buy you supper. I'll be right there."

Other Books by Robin Merrill

GERTRUDE, GUMSHOE COZY MYSTERY SERIES
Book 1: *Introducing Gertrude, Gumshoe*
Book 2: *Gertrude, Gumshoe: Murder at Goodwill*
Book 3: *Gertrude, Gumshoe and the VardSale Villain*
Book 4: *Gertrude, Gumshoe: Slam Is Murder*
Book 5: *Gertrude, Gumshoe: Gunslinger City*

CHRISTIAN FICTION
Piercehaven
Windmills (Piercehaven Book 2)
Trespass (Piercehaven Book 3)
Shelter (featuring Gertrude)
Daniel (the sequel to *Shelter*)
Grace Space: A Direct Sales Tale (the original Gertrude story)

DEVOTIONALS
The Jesus Diet: How the Holy Spirit Coached Me to a 50-Pound Weight Loss
The One Year Inspirational Words of Jesus for Women

POETRY
Almost Touching: new and selected poems